BEAR ATTACK!

Jessie watched with a mixture of amazement and disgust as her brother stirred the macaroni and cheese over the campfire. Maybe I'm not so hungry after all, she told herself.

Sean held up a clean fork and spoon. "Choose your weapon," he said grandly.

Jessie took the fork and tried a small bite. Her eyes widened, and she took a much bigger bite. "This is really good," she said.

"I told you," Sean said proudly. Then he stopped eating and jerked his head up. "What's that?"

Both of them saw it at the same time—shimmering bands of red, gold, and green light rippling across the night sky.

"The northern lights," Jessie whispered. "Isn't it awesome?"

Before Sean could answer, a dark figure moved out of the shadows and mounted a boulder. For a heart-pounding moment the huge shape stood outlined against the flashing northern lights like some creature from outer space.

Then suddenly it leaped down and charged at them!

ALASKA

A novel by Frank Lauria
Based on the motion picture written by
Andy Burg & Scott Myers

A MINSTREL® BOOK

Published by POCKET BOOKS
New York   London   Toronto   Sydney   Tokyo   Singapore

This book is a work of fiction. Names, characters, places and
incidents are products of the author's imagination or are used
fictitiously. Any resemblance to actual events or locales or per-
sons, living or dead, is entirely coincidental.

A MINSTREL PAPERBACK *Original*

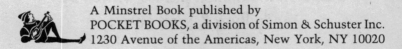A Minstrel Book published by
POCKET BOOKS, a division of Simon & Schuster Inc.
1230 Avenue of the Americas, New York, NY 10020

Copyright © 1996 by Castle Rock Entertainment

ISBN: 0-671-00178-7

First Minstrel Books printing August 1996

10 9 8 7 6 5 4 3 2 1

A MINSTREL BOOK and colophon are registered trademarks of
Simon & Schuster Inc.

Printed in the U.S.A.

For Anne Greenberg and Ellen Smith—
who keep the flame burning . . .

ALASKA

at the dazzling wall of majestic peaks and crystal ice spires across the clear sky. The splendor of Alaska's natural glory always filled him with awe.

Too bad his son, Sean, didn't see it the same way.

"Quincy Air Service to Super Cub Niner Zero Niner Tango." The crackling radio voice broke through Jake's thoughts. "Do you copy?"

"Roger that, Charlie," Jake said, fixing his headset. "Read you crystal clear."

"How was Nome?"

"Balmy," Jake answered. "They were having a heat wave. Almost hit freezing."

Charlie began to chuckle. "Sounds good. What's your ETA? You still on schedule?"

"You bet." Jake checked his watch. "My ETA is around seventeen hundred hours. See you then, Charlie. Cub Niner Zero Niner Tango clear."

"See you in a couple of hours, partner. This is Quincy Air Services, clear."

As Jake tugged on the stick, the plane lifted higher and banked steeply toward home.

Far below on the frozen earth the giant polar bear waited until the sound of the plane faded away. Then she nudged her cub and padded off in search of food.

As usual, the bear cub found it hard to keep up with his mother. There were so many interesting things to play with along the way. Chasing birds was always fun, and he liked the minty smell of dry pine-cones. But today he found something new—a chunk of ice.

The bear cub was amazed at how far and how fast ice could travel. Just one small tap of his paw would

3

send the heavy slab spinning across the ground. Chasing after it was the best fun of all.

Suddenly it was too quiet. The cub didn't notice, but his mother stopped and raised her powerful body. An enemy was watching them. She could feel it.

More than five hundred yards away, a tall man with hard, deep-set eyes adjusted his rifle scope. There in the crosshairs stood the largest polar bear he had ever seen.

For a long moment the hunter kept the bear in his sights. He watched the fierce animal turn her head as if she knew two men were hidden behind the rocks.

Very slowly he squeezed the trigger. Then he relaxed his trigger finger and looked back. His guide, Koontz, was coming from the sleek Bell Jet chopper parked on the ridge.

The hunter, whose name was Perry, pointed at the huge polar bear below. "Outstanding, Mr. Koontz. She must go eight, nine hundred pounds at least," Perry said quietly.

"More like nine-fifty," Koontz grunted. "Ain't she a beauty?"

Perry squinted at the powerful white beast through his scope. "Magnificent creature, the polar bear. Nature's perfect carnivore. Adapted to the most hostile climate on earth."

The burly, unshaven guide wiped his mouth. "Oughta fetch us ten, maybe twenty grand, just for the skin. God, I love this kinda huntin'."

Perry gave him an annoyed glance. "The trouble with you, Mr. Koontz, is you have no appreciation for the finer things in life."

He returned to his rifle scope and locked the crosshairs on his target. "Hunting is when you don't use a helicopter. Hunting is when you don't have to put up with people such as yourself. No. This"—Perry paused to lever a shell into the chamber—"is business."

He squeezed the trigger.

The shot blasted the silence.

The bear cub's furry body jerked with fright. He had heard thunder before, but this was different. Instinctively he looked around for his mother.

She was standing a few yards away, swaying from side to side. Her great claws were spread as if she were fighting off an invisible attacker.

Confused, the bear cub crept closer. He saw his mother turn toward him. Her fanged jaws opened, but she made no sound. Slowly she toppled to the ground.

A deep quiet settled over the icy hill.

CHAPTER 2

Jessie Barnes lifted her paddle and let the kayak drift. The bay was as smooth as glass clear to the shore. She could see the snow-capped mountains reflected on the surface.

Just ahead, the gleaming granite rocks were swarming with sea lions. The rocks had been polished and shaped by a thousand years of crashing waves. But today the only ripples in the water came from the kayak just behind Jessie.

As Jessie turned, her friend Chip's kayak floated up beside her.

"Why did you stop paddling?" Chip asked.

Jessie shrugged. "I wanted to check out the rocks where the sea lions live."

"What we call a rookery," Chip said.

Jessie smiled to herself. Chip had spent all thirteen years of his life in Alaska. He knew about the fish, the birds, and the hidden lakes. He shared his lore with Jessie, who was a year younger, but he never made her feel like a dumb city girl.

She gazed past the rookery to the fishing village that seemed to grow out of the water. Houses on stilts, docks on pilings, two-masted fishing boats—all were draped with ragged nets.

Welcome to Quincy, Alaska, Jessie thought. About as deep in the middle of nowhere as you can go and still have a zip code.

Funny thing was, Jessie didn't mind at all. She liked Alaska as much as her father did. It was Sean who was having the problem. . . .

Jessie pushed the thought of her brother aside and waved her paddle. "Race you back to shore."

"Think you can handle it?" Chip asked coolly.

"Well . . ." Jessie hesitated. "It is a long way."

Suddenly she shoved her paddle into the water, splashing him. The unexpected motion nearly capsized his kayak. As Chip struggled to steady himself, Jessie giggled and began paddling away.

"Last one back buys the ice cream," Jessie called over her shoulder.

"I want to start again," Chip shouted, taking off after her. He expertly worked his paddle to catch the current and leaned into it.

Up ahead, Jessie was paddling furiously toward the rickety docks. Her arms began to ache, but she ignored the pain. She focused all her attention on a sandy area between the piers as she kept churning water.

Even before she saw Chip's kayak, Jessie sensed him coming up behind her. Then she saw him from the corner of her eye, his paddle moving smoothly. She gave him a breathless grin as the bow of his kayak came up to hers.

Her grin was washed away by the cold water Chip flicked into her face as he passed.

"Now we're even!" Chip yelled.

Laughing and huffing for breath, they guided their kayaks to the small beach between the docks. Propped up against a work shed twenty yards from the water were kayaks of all sizes, shapes, and colors.

"I won!" Jessie sang out as their kayaks glided onto shore.

"You nuts?" Chip demanded. "Anybody could see I won."

"I saw it!"

The booming voice drew their attention. Jessie turned and saw a tall, black-haired man striding toward them. She recognized Chip's father, John Wood, who had built most of the kayaks displayed at the shed.

"I'd say it was a tie," Mr. Wood declared.

Jessie and Chip looked at each other. "Okay, tie," they said without enthusiasm.

"She's getting pretty good, Chip," Mr. Wood said, winking at Jessie.

Chip shrugged. "Yeah, not bad for a girl."

Jessie sprang out of her kayak, still excited despite being ankle deep in cold water. "We paddled out past the sea lion colony—I mean, rookery. And we surfed some waves out by the islands. It was awesome!"

"I don't know, Chip," Mr. Wood said dryly. "You must be some teacher. I think she's hooked."

Chip felt a faint glow of pride and something more. He wasn't sure he liked it. But he certainly liked having Jessie as a friend. The problem was, he didn't know how Jessie felt about him, and he was far too shy even to think about asking her.

Mr. Wood seemed to sense what was on Chip's mind. "Well, it's a good day to take a walk somewhere," he suggested. "You guys go on and have fun. I'll take care of the kayaks."

He leaned over and easily slid the kayaks onto the beach. "Just don't forget Grandpa."

His father's voice rang in Chip's memory as he and Jessie walked along the dock. Actually, he did want to forget Grandpa, at least for the next few days.

"Look at that."

Jessie's voice cut through his mood. She always lifted his spirits, even now, as she pointed at a net full of squirming red fish high above him.

"Salmon catch," Chip explained. "A few days ahead of season."

"Isn't that illegal?"

"I guess." Chip watched the boat's crane swing the load of fish down to the dock. "Poaching is big business out here. Fishermen, hunters . . ." His voice trailed off.

Jessie hadn't known Chip very long, but she could tell something was bothering him. Perhaps she could help.

"Hey, Chip," she said impulsively. "You want to come over tonight and have dinner with us?"

It worked. Chip's face lit up like a birthday candle.

"Well, yeah," he said casually, but there was a little bounce in his step.

Then the light blew out, and Chip's grin faded. "Aw, man, I can't. I gotta help my grandfather at the store 'cause we're leaving first thing in the morning."

Jessie looked at him. The worried expression was back. "Where are you going?" she asked.

Chip squinted at the pelicans landing on the water. He wasn't sure Jessie would understand. He wasn't even sure *he* did. Finally he took a deep breath and told her.

"We're going on a caribou hunt," Chip said carefully. "Everybody goes this time of year. My grandfather, my uncles, my cousins . . ." Chip struggled to find the right words to explain the ways of his people.

What he wanted to tell her was that all the male members of his family went on a ceremonial caribou hunt. It was a tribal tradition that went back countless generations. Chip also wanted to explain how important it was that he pass the test. Just the thought of failing made a tight knot in the pit of his stomach.

Rather than show fear, Chip forced a smile. "It's like this . . . ritual. I go out a boy and come back a man."

"Good," Jessie said softly.

Chip was somewhat surprised by her reaction. He couldn't figure out if she really understood or if she was just trying to be nice.

He stopped and looked at her. "I'd rather just stay home and watch TV," Chip confessed.

As soon as he spoke, Chip felt his face redden with

embarrassment. But he was saved by the bell. Or rather, by the beep of Jessie's watch alarm.

"Oh, my gosh, I'm late," Jessie said frantically.

"Late for what?"

Chip's question hung suspended like a balloon as Jessie turned and started running. "I'll see you when you get back, Chip," she called over her shoulder.

Confused but relieved, Chip watched her sprint away. It was just as well, he told himself. This trip with Grandpa was something he had to face on his own. Like a man.

The broad-shouldered seaman standing on the bridge of his boat scowled as the fishing vessel at the end of the dock unloaded its salmon catch.

Captain Burl knew the salmon were illegal, but he wasn't the sort to inform the authorities. That wasn't his way or that of the other hardy seamen who fished the local waters. No, Burl had his own business to mind and his own catch to unload.

He turned his attention to the crane being operated by his first mate. His fishing trawler was a fine, seaworthy craft, but the crane's mechanism was tricky. It had to be handled just right. And today's load was extra heavy—nearly a ton of wriggling sea fish.

Using hand signals, Burl guided the metal container up from the deck. As the crane's long boom swung around and began to lower the container, Burl saw a flash of movement.

Some fool was running full tilt along the dock. A second later Burl recognized the young Barnes girl. She was racing recklessly, hurdling ropes and hoses, dodging anything in her path.

With a sinking feeling Burl realized there was one thing Jessie couldn't dodge. She was sprinting directly into the path of the heavy metal container swinging down from his boat.

In a moment the container would slam down on her.

CHAPTER 3

"Yo!" Burl shouted, lunging for the winch handle. He grabbed it and yanked back hard.

Twenty feet below, Jessie was racing toward home, unaware of the danger from above. Suddenly a huge shadow swooped into view.

On reflex Jessie ducked. She felt a cool breeze brush the back of her head and kept running.

Up on the bridge Burl was relieved to see the metal container jerk to a stop. "Hey, watch it, Jessie!" he called, but she was already on her way.

"Yo, Cap'n!"

The mate's warning turned Burl's relief to dismay. The sudden stop had tipped open the container, spilling hundreds of slippery fish across the dock.

Mrs. Ben swept the wood-planked walkway in front of her general store twice a day. Her husband, Ben, liked to joke that his wife was practicing to fly away on her broom.

Mrs. Ben had to admit that the old-fashioned broom with its long wooden handle did look like a witch's Jet Ski, but all the native women in Quincy used the same kind.

Without warning, a figure loomed in the corner of her eye. Mrs. Ben froze as the figure leaped over her broom handle.

"Hi, Mrs. Ben," Jessie called out as she raced past the general store.

Ben appeared at the doorway, his wrinkled face set in general disapproval of the younger generation. "That girl is always in a hurry," he muttered, shaking his head.

Mrs. Ben smiled knowingly. "Must be noon." She lifted her broom and pointed at Jessie's retreating figure. "Boots!" she shouted.

Jessie darted down the gangway to a stilt house on the water. She stopped at the door and hopped around on one foot, then the other, removing her wet boots.

Barefoot, Jessie rushed inside the simply furnished house and plopped down in front of an elaborate aviation radio set that took up most of the den.

Jessie rocked back on the worn leather chair, checked her watch, and began flicking switches on the radio. At the same time she studied the aviation chart above her.

"Three, two, one . . ." Jessie counted down, then pushed the power switch. Immediately the radio crackled to life.

"This is Super Cub Niner Zero Niner Tango to Home Fire. Do you read me? Over."

Jessie beamed with pride as her father's voice came over the big speaker. She jammed a chunk of bubble gum into her mouth, picked up the microphone, and clicked in.

"You're right on time, Dad," Jessie drawled.

Even over the radio her father's tone was familiar. "Aviator rule number one . . ."

"A pilot sticks to his schedule," Jessie recited, popping her gum. She peered at the map. "What're your numbers?"

"Left Nome at 11:55. Course 170 degrees magnetic. Average air speed 120 knots. Winds aloft: estimate 25 knots from 277 degrees."

Jessie picked up a long ruler and measured an angle on the large map of Alaska above the radio. Then she punched the numbers into an aviation calculator.

When she got the result, Jessie popped another bubble and went back to the map. She ran her finger down the long ruler until she found her father's exact position.

She clicked on the radio. "You should just be hitting Devil's Thumb," Jessie told him.

Two hundred miles away, soaring over the jagged, snow-covered mountains, Jake Barnes smiled. His daughter had become a first-rate navigator.

"That's a roger," he confirmed. "Devils Thumb dead ahead."

Rising up before his windshield was a high, craggy tower with a sharply pointed peak. The mountain dwarfed all the other peaks around it.

As Jake flew closer, the Super Cub looked like a

yellow bee buzzing up to the walls of an immense ice castle.

"I suggest you go around it."

Jessie's voice came though loud and clear. Jake had been tempted to hop over the massive peak, and his navigator knew it.

Jake grinned and clicked on. "Whatever you say, sweetheart. Dinner smells good from here. Is your brother helping you like I asked him to?"

"That's a big negative, Niner Tango."

Jake's grin faded. "Where is he?"

Jesse hesitated. She popped a bubble and decided to go easy on her brother. "My guess is he's probably out shooting the rapids or wrestling grizzly bears. You know, just being the Alaskan mountain man we know and love."

Jake didn't smile at Jessie's little joke. Sean was having a slight problem adjusting to life in the wilderness.

At that moment Sean Barnes was trying to survive a vicious attack.

There were two of them: a hairy giant named Bigfoot, who had a club, and a nasty catlike beast called a weretiger who could destroy him with one bite.

Sean carefully circled them, ready to jump. He eyed the rocky ledge behind him. His timing had to be perfect. He patted his lucky Chicago Cubs baseball cap, faked left, and leaped right.

Bigfoot swung and whacked Sean with a surprise shot that tripped him up. Sean barely made it to the ledge. He hung there by one hand, then dropped into the bottomless pit.

16

"Game over!"

Sean slapped the control board in disgust and checked his score: 570,000. A hundred thousand below his personal best. In Chicago he was Streetfighter champ of the Citylights Arcade. These days he was just another fish out of water, Sean thought glumly. This sleepy general store was the hottest spot in Quincy.

He wandered past the shelves stocked with everything from potato chips to shotguns. When he reached the window he stopped and glanced outside.

Not yet.

Sean sighed and paced around the store, listening to the country music wailing on the tinny radio. The singer missed his girl. So did Sean. He also missed Wally, his best friend.

He caught a glimpse of himself in a dusty mirror. With his pale, freckled skin and his Chicago Cubs cap jammed down over his hair, no one would mistake him for a native Alaskan. At thirteen he didn't belong anywhere.

Sean moved through the aisles, only half aware of the canteens, tools, fishhooks, rain gear, rock CDs, and cookies stacked on the shelves.

On one counter was a display of handcrafted figurines, all of them bald eagles. In a way the counter was almost a shrine to the magnificent bird. Sean looked at the bird figures without really seeing them. He moved to the window and stared out at the bay.

A strange rustling sound caught his attention. Casually he looked over his shoulder. For a frozen moment he gaped at the terrifying face that loomed above him.

The creature's bony beak was as sharp as a hatchet, and its fierce eyes glared at Sean with hatred. Sean stumbled back, heart pounding with surprise and fear. Perched at the end of the counter was a live bald eagle!

A rack of potato chips blocked Sean's escape. He was trapped between the rack and a large shelf.

With an ear-piercing screech the eagle unfolded its great black wings and flew straight at Sean!

CHAPTER 4

"Squuuaaaawwwkk!"

Sean covered his head and backed into the shelf, nearly dumping everything to the floor.

Ben looked up from sorting the mail.

"Don't worry. His squawk is much bigger than his bite," Ben said dryly.

"I wish you would leave that bird at home," Mrs. Ben scolded.

Sean ducked as the eagle flew through the store, flapping its wings, stirring up magazines and greeting cards, before landing on the wooden counter next to Ben.

"You can't keep a small dog or a parakeet?" Mrs. Ben asked, straightening out the mess.

"Don't say that in front of him," Ben warned with a sly grin. "You're making him hungry."

The shopkeeper patted the eagle's head, then

reached into his pocket and fished out a can of meat. He peeled back the tin lid, picked out a scrap of meat, and tossed it to the eagle.

One quick snap of the bird's sharp beak and the meat was history. The eagle gobbled it down with obvious relish.

Fascinated by the close-up view of this wild, predatory bird, Sean almost forgot why he was hanging out. Then he noticed Mrs. Ben rearranging the greeting cards, and he remembered.

"Uh, can you just sort out any mail for me from Chica—"

Before Sean could finish his sentence, the eagle fluttered its wide wings, scattering the letters everywhere.

"Hey!" Sean yelled. This was definitely not his day. Sighing, he scooped some letters off the floor and checked the return addresses. Nothing from Wally.

Ben took the letters from Sean and leaned closer.

He pointed his thumb at the eagle. "He was there, you know," Ben whispered.

Sean made a face. "Where?"

"In the great fires of 1935 up on the Yukon River."

"You're getting younger," Mrs. Ben commented. "Last week it was 1929."

"I was a very young man hunting alone when the forest fire jumped the ridge," Ben went on calmly. "The winds were high, and the flames were moving faster than I could run. There was no way out of the firestorm, and I prayed to die quickly."

Mrs. Ben rolled her eyes. She had heard it all before. Sean half listened to the tale, his eyes on Ben's weathered hands as they slowly sorted the letters.

"Then I looked up, and through the smoke I saw an eagle flying in a circle." The old man stepped closer to Sean. "Something said to me, trust the eagle. Well, he flew through the smoke, and I followed. The heat seared my face. My feet burned, but I kept looking at the eagle until the sky was clear and the fire was behind me."

As Ben moved nearer, Sean edged back, his eyes still on the pile of unsorted mail. The old man shrugged, and picked up some letters.

Sean glanced at the eagle doubtfully. "You've been watching too much TV. He was just trying to get away from the smoke, that's all."

He was sorry he'd mentioned it, because Ben stopped sorting the mail and stood there, eyes wide, mouth half open, as if he'd never thought of that possibility before.

Ben turned to the eagle. "Was that it? You were trying to get away from the smoke? And all this time I thought you were my *tornak*."

"Tornak?" Sean repeated.

"He means, his pet," Mrs. Ben said.

"My spirit guide," insisted Ben. "He's free to leave any time he likes."

Sean wished he could say the same. "You got any mail for me or not?" he prodded.

Ben ignored Sean's rude tone and calmly sorted the last of the letters. He gave Sean an understanding smile. "Sorry. Not today, Sean."

Watching Sean leave, Ben couldn't help feeling sad for the boy. It wasn't easy to leave friends behind, he told himself.

*   *   *

21

As Sean stomped out of the general store he was sure Ben was making fun of him. He's probably hiding my letter, Sean fumed. He swung the door open just as somebody was coming in.

Sean recognized Jessie's pal Chip, but he was too angry and disappointed even to say hello. He shouldered past Chip and marched down to the dock.

"Hey, what's the matter with him?" Chip asked nobody in particular.

Ben shook his head, watching Sean's retreating figure through the window.

Sean continued along the dock, hands deep in his pockets, totally depressed. All around him it was business as usual in Quincy, Alaska.

Trawlers were unloading their catch. Crates of ice were being packed. Fishermen were making deals with mountain men. Native women, carrying their babies in slings, were shopping. And they all had one thing in common.

None of them noticed the city boy from Chicago dragging his feet along the planks.

Back home Sean would have been doing lots of exciting things with Wally, like skateboarding to the arcade or catching a rock concert. He felt like a castaway on a desert island whom nobody wanted to rescue, least of all his father and sister. Jessie and his dad seemed to fit right in with the local people.

Up ahead Sean noticed some teenagers getting ready to go out fishing. The two boys were about his age, and the girl was younger. They were laughing and talking as they grabbed their gear and tossed it into a leaky old rowboat as if they were going somewhere really special—like a night game at Wrigley

22

Field. Here in Alaska I can't even watch the Cubs on TV, Sean brooded.

In frustration, he kicked over a fish bucket. It contained nothing but water, which splashed harmlessly over the wet planks, but kicking it made Sean feel better somehow.

Spotting a small trash container in front of the fueling station, Sean turned and kicked it hard—karate style. His kick caught the container square in the center. As it rolled over, a big red can popped out of the trash, spilling shiny black motor oil everywhere.

At the same time a gust of wind lifted the baseball cap off Sean's head. He lunged after it as it tumbled to the ground, afraid the cap would land in the spreading oil.

Sean snatched it up and angrily brushed dirt off the Cubs logo.

"It's no use," Sean muttered to himself. "I'm stuck in the boonies."

"Well, you're stuck in something."

The booming voice made Sean jerk his head up. When he saw the state trooper his heart sank to his shoes.

"But trust me," Sergeant Grazer added grimly, picking up the spilled oil can. "It ain't the boonies."

CHAPTER 5

Jake Barnes eased his Super Cub lower as he passed Devils Thumb. Directly ahead was a flat wall of cliffs.

This is the tricky part, Jake told himself, checking his compass.

A moment later he saw a narrow gorge that formed a natural gate in the cliff wall. One side of the gate was a gleaming mass of ice; the other side was sheer granite.

Keeping a light touch on the controls, Jake approached the narrow gorge. He tipped the right wing, and the Super Cub sideslipped through.

As soon as the Super Cub cleared the gate, Jake increased his airspeed. He veered through a mammoth fjord, skimming over choppy green water. From his cockpit he could see the jagged tips of icebergs drifting like shark fins.

Jake smiled. Alaska was everything he had hoped

24

it would be, and more. Every day he discovered something spectacular. He banked the Super Cub and headed out over the Coastal Sea. He buzzed past islands thick with trees. Minutes later he spotted Quincy through his frozen windshield.

But when Jake began his approach, he felt a strong crosswind slapping at his wings.

As soon as Charlie heard the Super Cub's engine he stopped tinkering with his A-Star helicopter and trudged over to the landing dock, his eyes scanning the sky. He made out the stubby yellow shape of the Super Cub across the bay.

It was coming down fast, Charlie thought. Maybe he should move his A-Star off the helipad. Too late, he decided. Better to keep an eye on Jake.

Charlie zipped up his worn air force flight jacket and watched the Super Cub's wings rocking back and forth in the cold, hard crosswind. The plane looked like a boxer ducking and feinting as it came closer.

Just when it appeared that the Cub would overshoot the landing area, Jake made a move Charlie had never seen before. Instead of fighting the rough crosswind whipping up the water, Jake Barnes brought the Super Cub almost straight down.

The sturdy Cub seemed to stop in midair and hover like a yellow pelican before its pontoons gently hit the water. Jake expertly guided the plane toward the landing dock, its floats churning up water as it slid to a stop.

As Jake popped open the door, Charlie tied the plane to the dock with a rope.

"Nice landing," Charlie called. "That's a stiff crosswind."

Jake Barnes hopped onto the dock. "Any landing you can walk away from is a good one."

Charlie grinned. Jake was all right for a city fellow.

"That's what Amelia Earhart said—right before she and her airplane disappeared," he joked, helping Jake unload the cargo.

Jake gave Charlie a quick smile, then tossed him a case of coffee beans. "Let's see what we've got here," he muttered.

As they continued unloading cases onto the dock, Charlie's curiosity got the best of him. "Don't you ever miss it?"

Jake squinted at Charlie. "Miss what?"

"You know, the big-city action?"

Jake stared out across the bay. "If you're asking, do I miss being stacked up ten planes deep over O'Hare? No, thank you. I can truthfully say I don't miss it."

Charlie studied him for a moment, not quite convinced.

Suddenly uncomfortable, Jake ducked back into the plane. Charlie's question had stirred up too many memories. As he checked the cockpit, his eyes fell on a photograph taped to the dash.

It was a picture of a beautiful young woman with Sean and Jessie. The woman was Jake's late wife, Dawn.

Jake stared at the photo. When Dawn died, he had decided to make the big move north. It was a dream they had shared for a long time.

Jake roused himself from his thoughts and gave the plane a final check. Only one big box was left. He yanked the case outside.

"All in all," Jake announced, "what pilot wouldn't

be satisfied with the important work he does for his community?"

He plopped the large cardboard case onto the dock. It landed at Charlie's feet with a dull thud.

A wide smile creased Charlie's weathered face. The box was filled with rolls of toilet paper.

"The citizens of Quincy are forever in your debt," he assured Jake.

Just then the phone on the landing dock rang. Jake grabbed the receiver and took the call. "Hello? Yeah, this is Jake Barnes." His face clouded. "Sean did what?" he asked slowly. "Yes, of course. I'll be right down."

Even the police station in Quincy looked bogus to Sean. It was nothing but a big drafty room with a few wanted posters on the wall and a ham radio.

They sure could use a computer, Sean thought as he watched Florence, the secretary, peck out her report on an old manual typewriter. He wondered if there were real jail cells in the back.

Nearby, a short, balding trooper named Harvey had his feet up on his desk and kept spitting sunflower-seed shells into a trash can. Sergeant Grazer stood at another desk, sorting through some papers.

Sergeant Grazer paused and glanced at Sean. "We got three notes here from your school. They say you haven't dropped by in over a week."

"It's not a school!" Sean blurted angrily. "It's a beat-up old trailer with a flag out in front."

Trooper Harvey raised his eyebrows and gave Sean a knowing smirk. "A truant *and* a vicious kicker of trash cans. Maybe we should cuff him to the dock with a sign: Big-City Juv-e-nile Delinquent."

Grazer chuckled. "Now, that *is* something folks might pay to see."

"Hey, I was *born* in Anchorage," Sean protested. "My dad was in the air force there till I was three."

"You? A native Alaskan?" Harvey's question ended with a plunk as he spit some shells in the can.

Sean nodded, his jaw set. Grazer stepped closer and looked Sean over. "Hold out your hands," he said finally.

As Sean held out his hands, Grazer gravely inspected them. He looked sideways at Harvey. "My wife would kill for hands this soft."

Sean angrily snatched them back.

"Well," Grazer continued with a sly grin, "at least you'll look like a *real* Alaskan by the time you finish scrubbing the oil off the dock—with this." He tossed a tiny toothbrush in Sean's lap.

Sean gaped at it in disbelief. "With *this?* It'll take forever."

Grazer gave him a somber nod. "Just long enough for you to appreciate the fragility of our delicate ecosystem."

Bummer, Sean thought, staring at the slim toothbrush. Then he glanced at Grazer and Harvey. The moment he looked at them the troopers burst out laughing. The joke was on him.

Sean's relief was short-lived. The door chime sounded above the general laughter. When Sean turned, he saw his father striding into the station house.

And he sure wasn't laughing.

CHAPTER 6

Sergeant Grazer's expression became serious when he saw Jake Barnes enter the station. Grazer had kids of his own, and he knew how the bush pilot felt.

"Hey, Jake," Grazer said quietly.

Jake looked hard at Sean. "Sorry about this, Sergeant."

Sean examined his fingernails, unable to face his father. An awkward silence filled the small police station.

Finally Jake spoke up. "Can he go now?"

The question hung in the quiet. Sean could feel everyone looking at him, but he was too embarrassed to lift his head.

"Go on." Grazer sighed. "Get out of here." With a backhanded wave he pardoned Sean.

Sean blinked, unsure of what to do. He looked at Florence, who gave him a sympathetic smile. Then he felt his father's hand on his shoulder.

"C'mon, Sean."

Reluctantly, Sean got to his feet. Still avoiding eye contact with his father, he shuffled to the door like a prisoner in a chain gang.

Once they were outside, Sean felt a lot better.

It was late afternoon, and their footsteps echoed across the now deserted docks. Jake walked slowly, lost in thought.

Playing hooky from school and kicking an oil can certainly weren't major crimes. But Sean seemed to be headed for bigger trouble, and Jake couldn't help blaming himself a little.

"I think I'm ready to go home now," Sean said, squinting up at the gray-streaked sky.

"We *are* going home," Jake said, but he knew what Sean meant.

"I mean Chicago. I hate it here."

Jake winced. He had been through this before with Sean.

"Look," Jake said patiently. "I know this move's been tough. But sometimes people just need to make a fresh start."

"Well, I didn't," Sean said sharply.

Jake had to admit his son had a point. However, it wasn't all that easy. There was Jessie to consider and his new aviation company. This was his chance to build a future.

When they reached the house, Jake paused.

Sean knew his father wanted to say something, so he leaned on the rail and stared at the tiny boats bobbing on the pale blue water.

"Stay with it, Sean," Jake said quietly. "It'll get

better. I guarantee it." Jake patted Sean's shoulder, trying to encourage him. "What did your mom say to you after you struck out ten times in a row that year?"

"Never give up. Never give up," Sean recited dutifully.

"Never give up," Jake chimed in.

Sean winced inwardly, having been through this routine too many times before. For his father's sake he repeated the phrase, but his heart wasn't in it. All it did was remind him of how much he missed his mom.

"Well?" Jake said. "Do I have to drag out the big batting trophy you won the next year?"

"That was Little League," Sean said flatly. "This is life."

Overcome by confusing emotions, Sean turned and hurried into the house. Behind him the sky darkened as a mass of black clouds swallowed up the sun.

As usual Jessie had dinner ready for Sean and Jake when they got in. And as usual it was poached salmon.

Sean had to admit Jessie was a pretty good cook, but she knew only three basic recipes—and two of them were for poached salmon.

Still depressed, Sean picked at his food while Jessie and their father dug right in, chatting as they ate. His father didn't mention his brush with the law, but Jessie seemed to know something was up. She gave Sean a wry smile. "I guess offering seconds would be a waste of time."

Very funny, Sean thought, ignoring her.

"The salmon is delicious, Jessie," Jake said, trying to lighten the mood. He reached into his jacket and took out two small packages. "I brought something for you guys. From Nome."

Jessie quickly opened hers, tearing away the tissue wrapping. Inside she found an Eskimo carving of a seal. She beamed with delight. "Thanks, Dad," she said, holding up the soapstone figure. "It's beautiful."

Curious, Sean unwrapped his package. His expression didn't change when he saw the object inside. What's one more disappointment on a monster bad day? he told himself.

"Oh, thanks, Dad. A compass." Sean set it next to his plate and watched the needle twitch toward his fork. "What am I going to do with a compass?"

"You might try finding your way with it, for a start," his father said quietly.

For a minute or so a thick silence filled the room. Then Jessie perked up. "Chip and I went kayaking all over the place today," she announced. "His dad says I'm really good."

"Ooh, big deal," Sean remarked.

Jake gave his daughter a big smile. "That's great, honey."

Jessie grinned and helped herself to more salmon.

Sean shook his head in disbelief. "What's wrong with you guys?"

"Don't start," Jessie warned—too late.

Sean slammed his fork onto his plate. "Dad, c'mon! You said we'd try it here and if it didn't work out for us as a family, we'd move back to Chicago. Well?" he prodded. "It's been six months."

"And?" Jake asked mildly, wishing he could put this off.

Jessie cleared some dishes, uncomfortable with the subject. She understood Sean's problem, but like her father, she believed her brother wasn't giving their new life a chance.

"Dad, you used to fly 747s," Sean reminded Jake with a trace of sarcasm. "Now you're delivering toilet paper."

Nice shot, Jake thought, a little embarrassed by the truth. He smiled and tried to figure out a way to explain. Then he saw Sean's angry glare and knew there was no way.

Sean stared at his father, waiting for an answer. He looked to his sister for support, but she pretended to be busy.

The ringing phone broke through the uncomfortable silence. Relieved, Jake quickly picked up the receiver.

"Hey, Charlie," he said, smiling at Sean. "Uh-huh, right." Then his smile faded. "They're completely out? Get the ampicillin from the clinic, and I'll meet you on the dock in fifteen minutes."

Jake hung up and began gathering up his flying gear.

"I have to make an emergency run up to the mine at Wainright," he explained. "They've got five kids laid up with pneumonia."

"Dad," Jessie groaned. "You just got home. It's getting dark."

"There's plenty of daylight left. Come on, Jessie. If you or Sean got sick . . ." Her father shrugged and headed for the door.

"Maybe I won't be here when you get back!" Sean

exploded. "Maybe I'll just buy myself a one-way ticket back to Chicago."

Jake shook off the threat. "I don't have time for this, Sean."

"Mom would have had time."

Sean's answer stopped Jake cold.

"She would never have moved us here in the first place," he continued, pressing his advantage.

"Stop it, Sean!" Jessie shouted.

"No!" He screeched his chair back and stalked toward his dad. "None of this would be happening if she were still here."

"But, Sean," Jake said quietly, opening the door, "she's *not* here. I'm sorry, but nothing you or any of us can do will change that. We all miss her just as much as you do, but we've got to get on with our lives as best we can. You know that's what she would have—"

"Well, I wish you had died instead of Mom."

Sean felt tears streaming down his face as the words rushed out of his mouth. He wanted to take them back, but it was too late.

His statement sliced through the air and stabbed Jake square in the heart. His face trembled with hurt and disbelief. Then he took a deep breath and collected himself.

"Jessie, I'll radio at nine tonight sharp. I'm taking Devils Thumb Pass."

Jake wanted to say much more, but he couldn't.

The slam of the door behind him was echoed by a boom of distant thunder.

CHAPTER 7

Jake kept squinting at the forbidding sky as he went through his flight check. Once in a while a flicker of lightning lit up the horizon.

Nothing really serious, Jake told himself.

Charlie loaded the last case of medical supplies onto the plane and secured the doors. "There's a bad storm brewing out there."

He nodded toward the mountain range far beyond the bay. Jake turned and saw black thunderheads billowing into the sky.

"I think I can sneak her through before it hits," Jake muttered, cranking up the engine.

Charlie didn't seem convinced as he shut the door and watched Jake taxi across the water.

Once the Super Cub was airborne, Jake circled back over Quincy, passing his house. He glanced down and spotted Jessie waving to him from the front porch. There was no sign of Sean.

But dead ahead a black mass of thunderclouds rolled over the mountains like boiling oil, and lightning cracked the sky.

Out over the islands the wind had begun to whip up harder. The rumbling thunder muffled the sound of a gray helicopter churning upstream.

The Bell Jet Ranger moved sluggishly, slowed by its cargo. A kennel-type cage dangled underneath the chopper. Inside was a live polar bear cub.

The cage spun in the heavy wind, tossing the frightened bear cub from side to side. Trying to escape, the cub poked his nose through the plastic bars. But outside there was nothing but a rushing blur.

Koontz guided the helicopter down very carefully, aware of the valuable cargo swinging below. He was also aware that Perry was riding shotgun and watching his every move.

Slowly, Koontz lowered the chopper until the cargo touched ground about twenty yards from their base camp. When Perry gave the signal, Koontz unhooked the bear cage and eased the Bell Jet down beside it.

A perfect landing, but Koontz's boss didn't seem to notice. Scowling, Perry grabbed his rifle and hopped out of the chopper. He walked over to the cage and peered inside, making sure his prize was safe.

The tall, powerful hunter studied the small bear huddled in the cramped cage. Afraid and alone, the cub began to whimper. He'll feel better after he eats something, the hunter decided. He saw Koontz leave the helicopter, dragging something behind him.

Grinning from ear to ear, Koontz held up the fresh

polar bear skin. "Figure it's a shame to separate mother and child." He snickered.

Perry ignored the sick joke. The cub whined softly and poked a paw through the cage, reaching out for his mother.

"We could plump him up a bit—then we'd have two furs to sell." Koontz smirked. "Mama bear and baby bear. Nice, huh?"

Perry shook his head, unable to conceal his dislike of his partner in crime. "You're a fool, Koontz."

Scowling, Koontz rolled up the bear skin. The cub whined louder and scratched at the cage, trying to stay close to his mother.

Perry bit down on a slim cigar and took out an antique lighter. The small flame lit up his square-edged face as he puffed the cigar and contemplated his prize catch.

"Do you have any idea what my contacts in Hong Kong will pay for a live polar bear cub?"

Koontz shrugged, but his greed was wide awake.

"Higher than you can count."

"I can count pretty high," Koontz snapped. "On both hands if I have to."

The glowing cigar lit up Perry's evil smile. "You'll have to."

His face darkened when he heard the deep buzz of an airplane coming up the gorge.

Perry dropped his cigar and motioned for Koontz to stay still. Neither man moved as they watched the yellow Super Cub pass overhead.

"It's nothing," Perry declared. "Just a puddle jumper."

Even so, he knew that bear poaching was a felony.

37

The hunter glared intently at Koontz. "Get that bear under cover. And put a net over the chopper."

Grateful for the privacy afforded by the rising storm, Perry headed for his tent.

Jessie half listened to the radio bulletins as she watched the rain streak down the windows.

"Henrietta, down in Ruby, says she got her moose," the voice announced. "The dogs are okay, and she'll be comin' up to fish camp next week. Weatherwise we got *serious* gale warnings for the Gulf of Alaska. High winds, rain—"

Disturbed by the news, Jessie shut the radio off. She popped some bubble gum into her mouth and sat down at the aviation radio.

For the fifth time in the last five minutes, she checked her watch. It was almost nine o'clock. She began to count down the seconds remaining. "Three . . . two . . . one!"

Jessie's watch beeped. Her eyes went to the big speaker, and she turned up the volume. She held the mike expectantly, waiting for her father to call in.

But all she heard was a jumble of static and the howling wind outside.

Alone in his room, Sean sat slouched in his chair, bouncing a Nerf ball off the ceiling. The driving rain drummed against the roof, and the windows shivered. Instinctively, Sean checked the clock.

Nine o'clock. Time for his father to call in.

Sean left his chair and inched open the door. He peered into the living room and saw Jessie hunched over the aviation radio.

Jessie clicked on the microphone. "Home Fire to Zero Niner Tango. Come in."

But the only sound coming from the speaker was a hissing crackle.

Worried, Sean edged inside the living room. A sudden bang broke the silence as the wind slammed the front door.

"Aren't you gonna do anything about that banging?" Sean demanded.

Jessie checked her watch: 9:05 P.M. She clicked on the mike and tried again. "Do you read me, Niner Tango?"

No response.

Sean suddenly felt nervous. He went to the front door and looked outside. As soon as he stepped out onto the deck, the cold, whistling rain pelted his face. A flash of lightning cut across the steely sky and rumbling thunder shook the ground. This storm is real big, Sean realized, his heart sinking.

The thought of his father's small plane trying to ride out the wildly gusting winds and heavy rains twisted in his belly.

Sean went inside and tugged the screen door shut, but he continued to stare across the wind-whipped bay, thinking about those last terrible words he'd said to his father: "I wish you had died instead of Mom."

Behind him, Jessie was repeating the call letters over and over, but the only answer was the eerie, crackling static that mocked Sean's remorse.

The swirling black clouds became thicker as Jake's Super Cub fought its way along the fjord. The conditions got worse as he approached the mountains.

The weather had turned violent at this altitude. A screaming gale whipped snow across the windshield, making it nearly impossible to see. Jake wrestled with the controls as the Super Cub was tossed around like a toy.

For a few seconds the window cleared, giving Jake a few fleeting images of jagged mountain cliffs behind ghostly snow clouds. He climbed higher in the gathering darkness and switched on the radio.

"Home Fire, do you read me? Over."

All he got was a rush of static. Jake turned up the volume, and a faint but familiar voice crackled in his headphone. "Dad . . . are . . . there?"

"I'm here, Home Fire," Jake said with a grim smile. "I have less than ideal visibility. I'm going to deviate from the flight plan—try another pass. Over."

Jake climbed higher as Jessie's voice barely broke through the roar of static.

"Say again, Dad? Can't hear you. Over."

Jake started to speak, then glimpsed the towering spire of Devils Thumb looming up in his windshield. He banked hard right, pulling the plane into a tight turn.

The plane barely avoided the mountain wall but went into a steep dive, driven by the howling wind. Like a surfboard rushing down a tidal wave, the Super Cub dropped into a canyon.

The narrow space focused the wind's force, pushing the Super Cub faster than Jake wanted. He pulled the plane up and was relieved to see open air around him.

A moment later the gusting wind blew him into another canyon, but this one was much tighter. Jake could see sheer ice walls on both sides of the plane.

Unable to control the Super Cub in the cramped space, he revved the engine and started to climb.

Jessie was holding the mike so tight that her hand was sweating. She leaned close to the radio, listening through the thick static.

"Dad! Are you there? Over!"

The sputtering static continued.

"Sean!" Jessie called out. "I think something's wrong with Dad."

"No kidding," Sean said from the doorway. Jessie was so intent on the radio she hadn't noticed her brother.

"He was there. I heard him," Jessie muttered, clicking on the microphone. "But he's not answering now."

Sean watched his sister press closer to the radio as if trying to get inside. "Zero Niner Tango," she repeated, voice trembling. "Do you read me?"

The turbulence above the ice canyon was intense, smacking the Super Cub with harsh gusts that shook the wings. Jake tapped the instruments with his fingers to make sure they were functioning. The compass needle was swinging wildly, and his altimeter seemed to be stuck.

Jake wiped the mist from the windshield with his sleeve, trying to get a visual bearing. He squinted outside through the misty snow clouds. For just a moment they parted. And Jake's blood froze.

A massive ice-patched mountain face rose up directly in front of him.

Jake yanked back on the stick, pulling up with all

his might. The wings shivered like paper as the Super Cub skidded up along the side of the mountain.

As the Super Cub strained to keep climbing, Jake heard the engine cough, and the plane went into a wicked hammerhead stall. For a second the Super Cub hovered in midair before it slowly tumbled over and began spinning toward the cliffs below.

"Mayday! Mayday! Niner Tango!" Jake yelled. But he couldn't be sure anybody heard him.

As the plane twisted out of control in the screaming gale, Jake saw the jagged peak rushing at him like an express train.

An instant later the blackness exploded.

"Dad? Is that you? Over!"

As Sean watched from the doorway, Jessie raised the volume, but the high-pitched static garbled whatever message there was. Suddenly the static reached a crackling peak, and it sounded as if someone was shouting. Just then the speaker clicked off to an ominous *shhhhhhh* sound.

Jessie turned to Sean and he shrugged, trying not to look scared by what he'd just heard.

But his effort failed. His face knotted with worry, Sean stood listening to the strange noise pouring from the speaker like electric rain.

CHAPTER 8

The northern lights danced and flickered in the vast night sky like shimmering strands of red, green, and yellow ribbon.

Sean heard the crunch of footsteps in the blackness and realized he was making the sounds himself as he moved through the snow, searching. He stumbled into a patch of dim light and stood listening. All he could hear in the deep stillness was his own ragged breathing.

Some instinct told Sean to turn around.

When he looked back, he saw the savage grin of a saw-toothed polar bear looming over him. Sean tried to scream, but the sound froze in his throat. He tumbled backward to the ground, one hand upraised.

Sean blinked his eyes open. Outlined against the sky was a strange but familiar figure. A weathered hand came down to help him to his feet. Then the figure pulled back the hood of his animal-skin coat.

It was Ben from the general store.

He gravely spoke in his native tongue. Sean couldn't understand him, but the words sounded like a warning.

Ben pointed at something in the shadows.

As Sean stepped closer, a giant white bear with red eyes clawed its way out of the darkness with a heart-stopping roar!

Sean bolted up in his bed, sweating.

His brain snapped awake from his nightmare as he sat up. Still somewhat confused, Sean checked his watch—3:30 A.M. Gathering his senses, he slipped out of bed. The storm was still raging outside, and the tiny house swayed and creaked in the punishing wind.

Sean went into the living room and saw his sister asleep on the couch. The fire had faded to glowing embers. The radio was still on, but there was no sound except the dull, endless hiss of static.

As Sean moved over to the fireplace, he heard the radio click to life. He paused and stared at the radio. It clicked again. Heart pounding, he hurried to the desk and grabbed the mike.

"This is Home Fire. Do you read me? Over. Dad, is that you?"

Sean heard a final click. Then a gush of static flooded the wind-lashed silence.

In the morning, sunlight broke through the gray clouds, but the damage had been done. The townspeople were out early picking up debris and checking their boats.

As Sean and Jessie quickly made their way along

the littered dock, they saw a fallen power pole. A gang of repairmen were noisily working on it.

It was also busy at the state troopers' office.

Sergeant Glazer tried his best to listen carefully to what Sean and Jessie were saying, but the office was a madhouse after the storm. Florence was constantly answering the phone while Trooper Harvey kept tromping in and out, loading emergency equipment onto the police truck.

Grazer wasn't quite sure he believed Sean and Jessie's story. From time to time he glanced at Florence to make sure she was hearing everything.

"The radio was all fuzz after that," Sean said, leaning forward in his chair. "Then it suddenly got louder and cut off."

Grazer nodded thoughtfully. "And you're sure you recognized your father's voice shouting?"

"Yes. Well, no." Sean looked at Jessie. "But . . ."

"But I had just talked to him," Jessie reminded him. "He was headed for Devils Thumb."

Grazer sighed. "A lot of people use that radio channel, Jessie."

"Dad didn't check in after that," Sean said sharply.

"Maybe he did, and you didn't hear it," Grazer suggested. But he knew he couldn't ignore what Sean and Jessie were saying. "Uh, Florence," he said finally.

Florence was already dialing the phone. Obviously she believed Sean and Jessie's story.

"Hi, Elvira, this is Florence down in Quincy." She winked at Jessie. "Did Jake Barnes come in last night?"

Her face clouded as she listened to the reply. "Did he make contact by radio at all?"

45

Grazer didn't wait for an answer. He picked up the radio mike and clicked in. "Super Cub Niner Zero Niner Tango, this is Quincy. Over." He checked his watch. "Zero Niner Tango, this is Quincy. Do you read? Over."

All he got was fuzzy static.

"Okay . . . Okay. Thanks." Florence looked at Grazer and shook her head sadly. "They haven't seen him."

Jessie's face fell. "Sergeant Grazer, please . . ."

As Florence hung up, Grazer gave Sean and Jessie a sympathetic smile. "All right, Florence," he said wearily. "Call Search-and-Rescue at Elmendorf."

Florence frowned. "After this storm? They'll be swamped. It'll be hours before they send a plane up there."

Jessie couldn't believe it. She was about to protest when her father's partner, Charlie, entered the station.

"Hey, Charlie," Grazer called. "You heard from Jake at all?"

Charlie shook his head. Both Jessie and Sean slumped dejectedly.

"That's why I came to see you," Charlie added.

Sean looked up. His face suddenly brightened as he realized what his father's partner was trying to say. Charlie was going to search for Jake himself.

The intense storm had swept the sky clean. Visibility was unlimited as Charlie's helicopter glided low over an ice gorge, then swooped over Coogans Glacier.

Trooper Harvey was riding shotgun, scanning the

46

area below with powerful binoculars. "I don't see anything," he said, eyes glued to the glasses.

Charlie veered the helicopter toward some distant mountains and radioed the news to the state trooper's office. "Quincy, this is Rescue One. No contact on Coogans Pass."

When the report came in, Sean was sitting on a folding chair in the state trooper's office, his head in his hands. He was too anxious to pay much attention to all the activity. But Jessie couldn't sit still. She made some distance calculations, punched the numbers into her flight calculator, then ran her finger over the map of Alaska.

"He should be just past there! Near Devils Thumb!" she yelled to Sergeant Grazer.

The sergeant looked skeptically across the room at her but raised the mike to his mouth and told Charlie, "Be sure to take a good look around the Devils Thumb area."

Charlie guided the chopper toward a junction of two canyons. He recognized the familiar spire known as Devils Thumb. At this distance the peak did resemble a thumb with a long, pointed fingernail, he thought. But it definitely didn't look like a place where a plane could land.

Trooper Harvey continued to scan the mountainsides through the binoculars. He strained to spot something—anything—that might be the downed Super Cub, but the area was desolate. With disappointment in his voice he finally said, "That's a big negative on Devils Thumb."

*   *   *

Sean and Jessie waited tensely for the next report from Charlie. When it came, it wasn't what they wanted to hear.

"Nothing but rocks and snow" was his news.

Sean jumped up from his chair. "No! He has to be there!" he yelled at Sergeant Grazer. "They're not looking hard enough!"

Sergeant Grazer was sure that Charlie and Harvey were doing their best, but he clicked the radio on and gave further instructions. "Why don't you guys take another pass—just to be sure."

Charlie's voice came over the radio. "Ah, roger that. We're getting low on fuel, but we'll give it another look."

Grazer hoped that would satisfy Sean and Jessie.

On the far side of Devils Thumb, deep inside a narrow pass walled by jagged rock, lay the snow-covered wreckage of the Super Cub.

The plane was perched on a cliff, its nose tilted downhill. Snowdrifts had formed inside the cockpit, blown in through the partly shattered windshield. There was a gaping hole where one door had been ripped off its hinges.

Jake lay sprawled across the pilot seat, his face streaked red with frozen blood. His blackened eyes were swollen shut, and his breathing was shallow.

Then the faint *thunk-thunk* of a helicopter fluttered through the deep quiet. As the sound grew louder, Jake stirred. He forced his eyes open. He couldn't see what was making it, but he knew that sound. It was Charlie's big A-Star chopper.

"Help! Help!" Jake called weakly.

Dazed, he tried to sit up and felt a fierce pain shoot up his spine. Grimacing with agony, Jake fumbled around the cockpit with his hand. A few painful minutes later his fingers gripped the flare gun.

But when Jake tried to make sure the gun was loaded, both shells dropped out. As he groped around blindly with stiff fingers, the sound of the flapping blades of Charlie's chopper grew louder and louder.

On the other side of the peak, Charlie's A-Star helicopter climbed higher. Trooper Harvey's view was obstructed by a jagged cliff. He shook his head, then clicked on his mike. "Sergeant, we've seen a soda can, an old boot, and a gum wrapper—but no plane."

Charlie tapped his fuel gauge, then clicked on his mike, too. "We're gonna continue searching on up toward Douglas and refuel. This is Rescue One, clear."

Back at the state trooper's office, Sean couldn't believe what he'd heard. As Charlie's voice came over the radio, he yelled, "No!"

The outburst brought Sergeant Grazer from behind his desk to where Sean was slumped in his chair. Jessie stood nearby.

The sergeant put his hand on Sean's shoulder and in his most authoritative voice said, "Sean, that'll do." Then in a more kindly tone he added, "Why don't you two go on back to the house. We'll call you when we've heard something. There's nothing you can do here."

Jessie took a step back. As frustrated as she was,

she realized the sad truth in what the sergeant had said.

Finally Jake's frozen fingers found one of the shells. Frantically he reloaded the flare gun, then stopped and listened to the sound of the chopper. After determining its position, Jake scooped out a hole in the snow-covered wreckage of his side window.

He peered out at the patch of blue sky, then slowly and painfully aimed the flare gun.

The *phoom* of the gun filled the tiny cockpit and echoed across the stillness. Jake saw the blazing flare arc high, then explode in a poof of smoke.

But as the smoke disappeared, Jake could hear the sound of the chopper fading into the thick silence.

Desperately Jake tried to pull his body up. An electric shock of agony shot up his leg. Jake screamed once, then passed out.

It was dark when Jake finally came to. He groped around until he found his flashlight. He kept it on for a few minutes while he located his parka and pulled it around him.

Thirsty, he ate a handful of snow. The cold liquid seemed to clear his head. Realizing nobody would try to find him until dawn, Jake tried to settle in for the long, freezing night ahead.

As he did, his yellow Super Cub teetered on the ridge above the steep cliff, dwarfed by the colossal peaks. The tiny light in its cabin window was the one spark of life in the immense, howling blackness of rock and ice.

CHAPTER 9

Sean was awake at first light. He dressed quickly and hurried out to the landing dock to continue the search for his father. He had hardly slept, convinced his father's plane was somewhere near Devils Thumb Pass.

When Sean reached the landing dock, he saw a light on in Charlie's office. As he came closer he could see his father's partner talking to another man. The door was partly open, and their voices carried clearly in the dawn quiet.

"Well, we can't just write him off," Charlie insisted.

The other man turned. Sean recognized Sergeant Grazer.

"We're not writing anybody off," Grazer said calmly. "But we have to face facts. Search-and-Rescue has made three trips up to Devils Thumb."

Sean inched closer to the door but remained in the shadows.

"You saw that storm," Sergeant Grazer reminded Charlie. "Nobody's picked up any signal from his emergency beacon."

Sean could see that Charlie wasn't convinced. The veteran pilot's lined face hardened into a stubborn scowl. "Maybe he set the Cub down somewhere to wait it out. Or—"

Grazer finished the thought for him: "Or that plane's in a million pieces on the side of a mountain."

Without thinking, Sean burst through the door. "I can't believe this!" he screamed.

Surprised, Charlie and Grazer whirled toward him.

"My father's a survivor! He'd *cling* to life, no matter what, and you guys are just going to give up on him."

Without waiting for an answer, Sean turned and bolted outside.

"Sean, wait!" Charlie called.

But Sean was running too fast to hear him.

By the time he reached the far end of the dock, he was exhausted, angry, and scared. He collapsed at the edge of the pier and sat there for a long time, hugging his knees.

Far in the distance, just clearing the clouds, was the familiar outline of a mountain range. Those were the snow-capped peaks where his father was lost. As Sean stared at the mountains he understood what he had to do. Slowly he got to his feet and marched back to his house.

Jessie was in the living room when Sean arrived. She was sitting on the floor, her back tight against the wall, in an upright fetal position. She had the aviation calculator pressed against her chest.

She lifted her head when Sean entered, but he didn't speak. He went directly to the kitchen and began rummaging for food, pulling down cans and boxes.

Sean quickly gathered a supply of food and stuffed it into a shopping bag. So far so good, he thought as he carried the bag to his room. He locked the door and went to his closet, sure that Jessie wouldn't guess what he had planned.

He pulled out his backpack and threw it on the bed. He followed that with a rolled-up tent and the other gear he had stored in the back of his closet.

After packing his gear, Sean went to the window and opened it. He threw his backpack out first, then climbed out the window and dropped to the ground. He picked up his pack and turned to start walking away—only to find Jessie waiting for him.

Jessie was carrying her own backpack with a climbing rope and other gear lashed to the outside. He'd been wrong, Sean realized. Jessie had figured out what he was up to.

"Where are you going?" she asked casually.

"Nowhere," Sean grunted, marching away.

Jessie fell in behind him. "For somebody who's going nowhere, you sure packed a lot of stuff."

Sean didn't slow down but nodded at Jessie's bulging backpack. "You're not exactly traveling light yourself."

Jessie gave him a superior smile. "*This* is stuff that might actually be useful in trying to find Dad." Triumphantly she waved the aviation chart and a pair of binoculars in her brother's face.

The gesture snapped Sean's frayed nerves. Embarrassed, he blocked her path. "No!" he yelled. "You're not coming with me."

Jessie marched right past him. "Why would I want to go with you?"

Sean hurried to catch up. "Jessie, you have to stay here."

"Who says?" she asked coolly.

"I do."

Jessie seemed surprised by his answer.

"With Dad gone, I'm the man of the house."

"Then stay in the house," Jessie declared. "I'm going."

Sean stopped. "Fine. I'll see you at Devils Thumb."

"No, you won't," Jessie said flatly.

"Why not?"

"Because you don't even know where it is." Jessie turned and pointed across the bay. "Because in case you didn't notice, we live on an island. What are you going to do, swim to Devils Thumb? Even if you get a ride on a fishing boat, with what *you* know, you'll die."

Sean eyed his sister with new respect. There was no denying she was right.

"What I *know* is that Dad's still alive," he said firmly. "He would survive out there. I can't just leave him, Jess. I gotta try."

Jessie met his gaze. "You'll never make it."

"You have a better idea?" Sean challenged.

Jessie flashed a proud smile. "Of course I do."

Sean had serious doubts about Jessie's brilliant idea. One look at the two-person kayak built by Chip's father was enough for him. The flimsy craft looked as though it might sink as soon as it got wet.

"What is this," he muttered.

"It's a baidarka—an Eskimo kayak," Jessie explained. "I've used it before with Chip. You can travel more than twenty-five miles a day in one of these."

She shoved the kayak into the water.

Might as well give it a try, Sean thought. Awkwardly, he climbed in the rear opening. Jessie took the front and handed him a double-bladed paddle.

The morning mists steamed around the kayak as Jessie and Sean paddled across the bay. Finally they emerged from the swirling cloud into brilliant sunshine. It hadn't taken long for Sean to get the hang of propelling the kayak. With him paddling swiftly in back and Jessie pulling in front they were making excellent progress.

Although Sean was tired, his eyes were wide open, as if he were seeing the world for the first time. They paddled past giant snow-topped mountains that were reflected in the clear water and wove a course around tiny islands choked with tall trees. Awed by the splendor around him, Sean dipped his paddle out of rhythm, and it clanked against Jessie's.

"One-*two*, one-*two*, one-*two*!" Jessie yelled. "Stay in sync!"

Sean took a deep breath and focused on his paddling with new determination, ignoring the breathtaking scenery.

After another hour they reached a rock garden jutting out of foaming water. Jessie suddenly stopped paddling.

Relieved, Sean slumped over, resting while his sister checked the compass. "My arms are killing me," he groaned. He wriggled in his seat. "And my butt is *really* killing me."

Jessie unfolded the map, which she had tucked into a self-locking plastic bag on the deck in front of her. She turned and pointed up the fjord, between two islands.

Sean followed her finger and saw giant waves crashing over sharp black rocks. Swirling just beyond the rocks were wild, treacherous currents roaring through a narrow gorge.

"We have to go through there," Jessie declared.

Sean's eyes went wide with fear and disbelief. "Now *you're* really killing me," he muttered, staring numbly at the raging waters ahead. "Can't we just go around?"

Jessie looked back at Sean. "Not without paddling like twenty-five miles out of our way. Dad flew up that fjord, and that's where we have to go." She pointed out their route on her map. "If we make it through the rocks, we'll paddle up the fjord as far as we can, then hike up the glacier to Coogans Pass and then across the mountains to Devils Thumb."

"If?" Sean's eyes went wide with disbelief. *"If?* What if we *don't* make it through the rocks?"

"Then we won't have to worry about getting up that mountain. Or finding Dad. Or explaining why we stole this kayak from Chip's father. We won't have to worry about anything," Jessie said, looking at the violent water ahead, "except how painful it is to drown in cold water."

Sean tried to appear calm. "Thanks, Jessie. I feel much better."

Jessie didn't seem to hear him. She was studying the swells again.

"Let's go—now!" she yelled. "Paddle!"

They began paddling at the same time. Pushing through the pain, Sean gave it everything he had. Suddenly they hit a strong current, and he felt the boat lift like an airplane.

"Ahhhhh!" Sean howled as the kayak swiftly cut across the foaming water toward the rocks where the waves were breaking.

Jessie leaned forward, her eyes fixed straight ahead and her arms paddling hard. A huge swell loomed in the corner of her eye, then curled over the small boat like a giant jaw about to snap shut.

"Uh-oh! Come on. Forward, hard!" she screamed above the roaring water.

Sean jammed his paddle deep into the water, but it was all foam. "Oh, nooooo!"

"Turn away from the wave!" Jessie yelled. "Left! Left!"

Desperately Sean dug his paddle into the roiling water just as the wave's crest began crashing down. "It's breaking!" he called out, trying to paddle in sync with Jessie.

"Go!" Jessie cried. "Go!"

Both their paddles hit the water at the same time and the kayak darted forward. The wave caught them perfectly, lifting their craft like a long surfboard, and they squeaked through a narrow gap between two rocks.

"Yes! Yes!" Sean whooped. "Ha-ha! Yahoo!"

A big grin spread across Jessie's face, but her eyes were scanning the rough waters ahead. "Paddle hard. We're not out of this yet," she warned. "One-*two!* One-*two!*"

They shot between two huge rocks like an arrow, catching a strong current that carried them high in the frothing water—then dropped them even faster.

Arms pumping together perfectly, Jessie and Sean both felt a surge of natural excitement as they sped past the rocks.

"That was incredible! It was like riding a rocket!" Sean shouted, lifting his paddle in triumph.

It was too soon to celebrate, though. By lifting his arms, he caused the kayak to wobble. Then, when Sean jabbed his paddle into the water, it hit a rock. The paddle flew out of his hands and fell into the water. Sean reached down to grab it.

"Sean! No!" Jessie warned, whipping around.

Without a sound the kayak overturned in the churning water. Both Jessie and Sean disappeared beneath the bubbling rapids.

All that could be seen of the kayak was the hull, bobbing like a cork—and Sean's paddle floating swiftly downstream.

CHAPTER 10

For a frozen moment there was nothing except the foaming rush of water. Suddenly a paddle blade broke through and sliced across the bubbling surface.

As if by magic, the kayak rose out of the water, righting itself, as Jessie executed an Eskimo roll, bringing Sean up with her. Both of them were soaked to the bone. Their bodies shook with cold, and they were gasping for breath.

"You idiot!" Jessie sputtered.

"I didn't tip us over!" Sean said breathlessly. "You did!"

Jessie controlled her anger. "Get the paddle," she directed. "We've got to dry out."

Cold, wet, and sore, Jessie and Sean reached shore and dragged the kayak onto the beach. Jessie threw down her paddle and grabbed for her backpack.

"Great," Sean muttered. He turned the kayak over to empty out the water. "This is really great."

Wishing her brother would stop complaining all the time, Jessie rummaged through her gear.

"We're going to freeze to death," Sean said, flapping his arms.

Jessie gave him a disgusted look. "What's the big deal? We'll build a fire."

"Good, I hope you brought the matches."

What do you think I'm looking for? Jessie was about to say—until she unzipped the last pocket and realized it was empty. She had left the waterproof match case on her bed, along with the extra batteries for the flashlight.

"Oh, no," Jessie groaned. She checked the other pockets again, but she knew it was useless. To her annoyance Sean seemed almost pleased.

"What do we do now, Pocahontas—rub sticks together?"

Furious with her brother, Jessie went through the backpack again, looking for a stray pack of matches. Her legs began to ache, and she sat down on the hard ground.

Then she saw it, coming from inland—a wispy trail of smoke drifting above the timber. "Hey," Jessie said. "What's that?"

Sean followed her gaze. "Looks like somebody who didn't forget the matches."

"Maybe they saw Dad's plane," Jessie said quietly.

She and Sean turned and looked at each other. A moment later they began walking quickly toward the trees.

It didn't take them long to find the source of the smoke—a deserted campsite. The camp was set up very well, but the campers had made a serious mistake. They'd left the campfire embers burning, and the wind had fanned up the flames.

Still soaking wet, Sean and Jessie slowly approached the small fire, looking around the empty site. Jessie noticed a gray helicopter parked nearby, covered with a camouflage net.

"Hello?" Sean called loudly.

No answer.

Sean turned. Several tents, fuel drums, and various other pieces of gear were neatly arranged and netted over so they wouldn't be seen from the air.

"Is anyone here?" Sean shouted.

The silence was almost eerie.

Jessie looked around. She could sense something close by. "I don't like this," she whispered.

Sean approached one of the tents. Cautiously he pulled back the flap and peered inside.

A pair of savage jaws yawned out of the gloom, sharp white teeth bared for action.

Instantly Sean's head snapped back and he stumbled.

"Arrgghh!" he yelled, falling to the ground.

"Sean!" Jessie rushed over and helped him up. At the same time she looked inside the open flap.

"I don't believe it," Sean said. He began to laugh.

Jessie didn't find it so funny. Hanging inside the tent was a fresh polar bear pelt. The bear's grinning skull stared out at them.

"That's a polar bear skin," she declared angrily. "That's illegal. You can't hunt polar bears in Alaska!"

Sean looked shocked. "Really? Why don't you write 'em a note, Jessie? Like 'Dear poachers, this is very, very bad. I'm telling.' "

Ignoring him, Jessie studied the dead animal. Such a magnificent creature, she thought. It had been murdered. No one had the right to shoot down a helpless beast. The bear had had no weapon and no chance of surviving.

"Let's get out of here," Jessie said. The camp gave her the creeps.

"Wait," Sean said. They still hadn't found what they needed. He moved deeper into the tent and saw a big stack of animal hides, walrus tusks, and caribou antlers. These guys are really dangerous, Sean thought. They kill everything in sight.

Sean suddenly spotted what he was looking for—a fancy old lighter left on a camp chair. Now they could dry out somewhere. Then he heard a weird cry.

"Dweeuh!"

The sound was half animal, half human. Sean grabbed the lighter and rushed outside.

"What was that?" Jessie asked, looking around.

"Dweeuh . . ."

This time Jessie could tell where the cry was coming from. She walked quickly between the tents.

"Jessie, come on," Sean warned. But his sister forged ahead. Reluctantly he followed her around the tent.

When Sean got there he found her crouched beside a metal animal trap made from a drainpipe. Cut into the side was a small window with a door. He could hear something furiously scratching inside.

"Jessie, what're you doing?" Sean yelled, too late.

Before he could stop her, Jessie reached out and unlatched the window.

Without warning a white snout popped out, sharp

teeth bared! Jessie and Sean yelped and tripped over each other, stumbling to the ground.

For a moment they remained still. Then they slowly got to their feet and peered into the trap.

Inside, pacing restlessly in his prison, was a plump bear cub.

"It's a baby polar bear!" Jessie exclaimed softly. She edged closer to the open window. The cub shuffled back into a corner.

Jessie smiled and reached out. "Don't be afraid. We're not going to hurt you."

"Get away from there, Jessie."

Sean's warning annoyed his sister. Jessie glared at him defiantly. "We can't just leave her. That's her mother hanging back there."

"What makes you so sure it's a girl?" Sean countered. "Come on, let's get out of here." He tugged at Jessie's arm. "What if those guys come back?"

"Dweeuh," the cub whined.

Sean paused and stared at the furry bundle inside the cramped cage. Its soft black eyes were wide with fright. The cub was helpless. In a way, he knew how the orphan cub felt. Sean looked at his sister and shrugged.

Jessie grinned. "A polar bear can travel fifty miles a day," she assured him. "The hunters will never find her."

Less than a mile away the powered Zodiac raft carrying the hunter, Perry, and his guide, Koontz, was making its way back to camp.

Neither man said anything, tired from the day's slaughter. But the pile of endangered-animal skins between them spoke clearly of the crimes they had committed that day.

The low buzz of the motor was the only sound as the Zodiac wove its way among the rocks. Although they had bagged more pelts than they needed, Perry kept his cold blue eyes on the shoreline—and held his hunting rifle close.

The hunter was ready to shoot whatever crossed his path.

CHAPTER 11

The main door of the metal cage was sturdy.

Jessie and Sean stood on top of the cage, both pulling together, but the door wouldn't give.

Curious now, the bear cub poked his nose through the window and cocked his head to get a better look.

They took a deep breath and tried again. Giving it all he had, Sean felt the door begin to bend a little. Jessie felt it too, and they kept tugging until they had made an opening big enough for the cub to escape.

Problem was, the cub didn't want to leave his cozy quarters. He sniffed at the opening, then flopped over and looked up at them.

"All right, polar bear, *run!*" Sean said, waving one arm.

Cautiously the bear crept out of the trap. But he didn't run away. Instead he stood up on his hind legs, placed his big paws on top of the cage—and yawned.

Jessie smiled. "She's not going anywhere."

Sean bent closer to the cub and pointed to the trees. "You can leave anytime now."

The bear cocked his head.

"Go! Run! You're free!" Jessie declared.

Sean was much less polite. "Get out of here! Get a job! Write us a letter! The bus is leaving!"

The bear stretched out its paws and tried to climb up next to them.

"Hey!" Sean warned.

He and Jessie darted to the other side of the trap to avoid the bear's sharp claws. Just then they heard the faint sound of a motor coming in their direction. Sean gave his sister an angry I-told-you-so glare.

" 'They'll never find her, Sean,' " he whined, mimicking Jessie. " 'She'll be fifty miles from here.' "

"What're we going to do?" Jessie asked nervously as the sound came closer.

Before Sean could answer, the bear hopped up on the trap and tipped it over, knocking Sean and Jessie to the ground.

"Run!" Sean grunted, scrambling to his feet. He reached out for Jessie, but she was already up and running.

Both of them sprinted back to their kayak as the sound buzzed louder through the forest. Not far behind, the bear cub scampered after them.

Struggling to stuff his legs into the kayak, Sean looked back and saw the bear straining to catch up.

"Well, he's got 49.9 miles to go," Sean said, lifting his paddle.

As the kayak glided into the swift current, Jessie

looked back. The little bear was standing knee deep in water, his expression forlorn.

When they were out of sight the bear turned back toward the poachers' camp and lifted its head. Suddenly it was quiet again. The cub caught the familiar scent of Koontz and Perry and froze.

Through the trees he glimpsed the two men pulling their raft onto shore. The hunters carried another scent with them—fresh blood.

Afraid, the bear cub softly padded into the forest and lost himself among the silent trees.

"We've been robbed!" Koontz exclaimed. He slammed the trap's damaged door shut and looked around. "I can't believe this. Isn't *any* place safe anymore?"

Perry, his jaw knotted with anger, knelt and studied the tracks in the ground. "There were two of them."

His guide looked nervous. "You don't think it was Fish and Game, do you?" Koontz said.

"No." The hunter shook his head gravely. "They would have taken everything." Perry stood up and looked around. "These were amateurs—very impolite amateurs."

Koontz shrugged. "Yeah, well, they're one bear up on us now." He began pulling the day's catch out of the Zodiac. "Let 'em have the bear cub. We've still got the biggest haul in three seasons. My chopper can hardly lift the skins alone."

Perry's eyes burned like blue flames as he glared at Koontz. "Refuel the Zodiac."

"Whoa," Koontz protested. "Wait a second. If you

think I'm gonna go traipsing all over Alaska just to find some bear cub . . ."

Perry didn't seem to hear him. "They left on foot," he said calmly. "They're not far from here."

"I don't care where they are," Koontz declared. "I'm not spending my time—"

"Your time is mine, Mr. Koontz!" Perry reminded him sharply. "I pay for it; I'll decide how to use it." The hunter stepped closer to Koontz and stared at him. "I want that cub."

Koontz took a deep breath, picked up his gear, and threw it back into the Zodiac. "All right. But don't expect pleasant company. I'm gonna be wicked irritable when I catch up with these guys."

"I'm counting on it," Perry said, his deep-set eyes bright with rage.

Bad news travels fast, Charlie thought as he walked along the crowded Quincy dock. The boats were in, and all the fishermen were talking about the missing bush pilot.

Emergency radio alerts had been broadcast by the Coast Guard and the Air Patrol. Charlie had been with Sergeant Grazer all morning, waiting for some word about Jake's plane.

There had been nothing so far. Charlie hadn't given up hope, but he knew that the first twenty-four hours were crucial to Jake's survival. Unfortunately it was impossible to mount a rescue mission without some idea of where Jake's Cub had gone down, so the Air Patrol had ended its search.

Charlie paused when he reached the Barnes house,

wondering how best to break the news to Sean and Jessie. Then he took a deep breath and knocked.

No answer.

"Hey, kids, it's me, Charlie," he called loudly. "I need to talk to you. . . . Hello?"

Through the window Charlie could see that the lights were still on inside. He tried the door and found it unlocked.

He stepped into the house. "Sean? Jessie?"

Receiving no answer, he walked through the deserted house, checking Sean's room, then Jessie's. On Jessie's bed he found a waterproof match case and some batteries.

Then he heard the gong of the mantel clock and went into the living room. No sign of life. But something was different. Then it caught his eye—the big empty space above the radio.

Jake's aviation chart was gone. So was the large map of Alaska that had been tacked on the bulletin board.

He glanced into the kitchen. The cupboard doors were wide open, and cans of food littered the counter. Suddenly he knew where Sean and Jessie had gone.

"Oh, no," Charlie muttered, hoping he was wrong. But when he checked Jake's room he saw mountain-climbing and camping gear all over the floor.

One thing was sure, Charlie thought grimly as he hurried back to Sergeant Grazer's office: wherever those kids had gone off to, they had forgotten to take matches.

The full moon outlined a lone wolf howling on a high ridge overlooking the great fjord. Far below, the

69

shadowy darkness was broken by a flickering orange campfire.

Sean and Jessie sat near the small fire, comfortable now in warm clothes. Just behind them their wet clothes hung on the side of the kayak, drying in the heat.

Sean reached into his backpack and held up a box of macaroni and cheese. "Dinner, chez Sean," he announced.

Jessie gaped in disbelief. "What're you going to cook it in—your hat?"

With a flourish, Sean produced an aluminum saucepan from his pack.

"It's the only thing I know how to make," Sean said, opening the box, "but I make it good."

He mixed the macaroni with some water from his canteen, then opened the cheese-sauce packet and stirred the goopy contents together over the fire.

Jessie watched with a mixture of amazement and disgust as her brother cooked dinner. Maybe I'm not so hungry after all, she told herself.

Sean took a clean fork and spoon from his pack and held them up. "Choose your weapon," he said grandly.

Maybe one bite, Jessie decided, taking the fork.

Sean carefully placed the pan between them. "All right. Stay on your side of the pan."

"Don't worry," Jessie assured him. She grimaced when he took a big spoonful of the macaroni and ate it. After making sure he wasn't going to die, Jessie tried a small bite.

Her eyes widened, and she took a much bigger bite.

Then another. "This is good," she said between mouthfuls. "This is really *good!*"

"I told you," he said proudly. "No one does junk food like Sean Barnes." Then suddenly he stopped eating and jerked his head up. "What's that?

Both of them saw it at the same time—shimmering bands of red, gold, and green light rippling across the night sky.

"The northern lights," Jessie whispered. "Isn't it awesome?"

Before Sean could answer, a dark figure moved out of the shadows and mounted a boulder. For a heart-pounding moment the huge shape stood outlined against the flashing northern lights like some creature from outer space.

Then suddenly it leaped down and charged at them!

"The bear! Ahhhh, watch out!" Sean yelled as he and Jessie scrambled away in either direction.

The young polar bear lunged between them and buried his face in the pan of macaroni.

"Oh, man." Sean laughed. "He'd better be eating off your half."

Sean stopped laughing when the bear licked the pan clean and then tried to bite into it. "Hey! Hey! That's our kitchenware!" he yelled. Losing all fear, Sean grabbed the pan's handle and wrestled it away from the bear.

Jessie hurriedly dug through her pack and pulled out a box of marshmallow pies. She shook one out, tore off the wrapping, and tossed it to the bear. Instantly the young bear snatched up the treat and scampered off into the shadows with his dessert.

"Great," Sean muttered. "That should keep him

71

away—for about ten seconds." He plopped down near the fire and held the other marshmallow pie out to Jessie. "Here. We'd better eat the rest before he gets back."

But as Sean noisily unwrapped the pie, crinkling the cellophane, Jessie heard something. She held up her hand. "Shh!"

Cutting through the dark silence came the faint buzz of an outboard motor. As they listened, it grew louder and louder.

"Oh, no," Jessie whispered. "That's the same boat—from the camp."

Both Sean and Jessie stared through the shadows that were dancing around their tiny campfire. All they saw was the deep blackness of night as the buzz became fainter and faded away.

Sean took a deep breath. "They kept going, thank goodness."

But as he looked up, he saw Jessie's face freeze with horror. Sean turned, and his heart stopped.

A tall, menacing figure was perched on the rocks behind him. A hunting rifle dangled from his shoulder, its metal barrel glinting in the dark. The man's face was masked by the shadows until he slowly came down into the firelight.

As the man came closer, his deep-set blue eyes seemed to burn into Sean's soul. Then he stopped. Behind his goatee, his scowl twisted into a cold smile.

"Mmm," he said mockingly. "Something smells good."

CHAPTER 12

Just a couple of dumb kids, Perry thought. They were terrified by the sight of him. For now he intended to keep it that way.

He stood just behind the boy, where he could keep both kids in sight. "Oh, no, go ahead," Perry told them. "Don't mind me. I've already eaten."

Sean and Jessie sat there, afraid to move. Without turning his head, Sean secretly scanned the darkness for the bear.

Perry came closer. "My partner and I saw your fire from the river. Well, I said, it just wouldn't be polite not to say hello."

"Hello," Jessie snapped.

"Hello," Sean added defiantly.

The kids have heart all right, Perry thought with admiration. But he was sure they were the ones who had raided his camp. He looked around and noticed their kayak. It was a beauty. Completely handmade.

"That's a fine-looking kayak," he said, watching their faces closely. "Don't see those native boats around much these days. Which way are you taking it?"

As he came closer, Jessie got up and backed away.

"Up-country," Sean said quickly.

"Oh!" Jessie exclaimed, bumping into a large stranger standing in the shadows. The stranger gave her a nasty smile and squatted next to her.

The man with the rifle acted as if nothing had happened. His deep-set eyes studied Sean's face. "If you came up the coast, you must have seen our camp."

Sean tried to keep his voice steady. "We didn't see anything."

The man with the rifle seemed amused. "Really?" he said calmly. "I find that difficult to believe."

Sean swallowed hard as the man's cold scowl melted into a sinister smile. "My name is Perry." He pointed to the other man. "This is my pilot, Mr. Koontz. And you are . . . ?"

"Jessie."

"Sean." As he introduced himself Sean noticed a metallic glint near the fire. His heart sank when he saw the fancy lighter he had taken from the hunters' camp. It was lying in plain sight.

"So, Jessie and Sean," Perry went on, "what's up-country?"

"Our father," Sean declared. The truth seemed to make his voice stronger.

Perry stared him down, unimpressed by his answer. "Really?" he murmured.

Jessie cringed as Koontz suddenly leaned over her

to grab something. The pilot grinned in triumph and held up the bear-bitten pan.

"My, my, Grandma," he rasped loudly, "what big teeth you have."

"And what powerful jaws," Perry added. "Did your dog do this?"

Even without looking, Sean could feel Perry's blue eyes drilling into him. Sean decided to face him, man to man. "A bear bit it," Sean declared.

"Really?" Perry said, glancing at Koontz.

Sean took a wild chance. "Right before my dad shot him." Instantly he wished he hadn't tried.

Koontz snorted. "Your dad shot a bear for biting his pan?"

"For interrupting his dinner," Sean snapped, refusing to admit defeat.

Koontz squinted at Sean and guffawed. The pilot's raspy laugh sounded strangely menacing in the silence of the dense forest.

Perry smiled and casually moved closer to the fire. Sean's stomach flopped over as the hunter bent down and picked up the lighter.

Calmly, Perry lit a cigar. "You know, Sean," he said slowly, "if there's one thing I hate worse than a thief, it's a liar."

Sean felt a trickle of sweat run down his neck.

Without warning, Perry turned and tossed the expensive lighter back to Sean. Caught off guard, Sean bobbled it a moment, then held on.

"A trade," Perry said. "For the bear cub." His face was like stone in the firelight. "Tell him to come home when you see him." He turned to Jessie and tipped his hat.

"Good night, young people. Don't be afraid of the dark."

Perry's sinister smile unsettled Jessie. She glanced at Sean, who seemed to be in shock.

When Jessie looked back, the two hunters had already disappeared into the darkness.

Koontz couldn't believe what had just happened. Muttering and shaking his head, he followed Perry to the Zodiac.

"I thought you wanted to"—Koontz imitated Perry's voice—*"get the bear."*

"They didn't steal it," Perry said, squinting through the shadows.

"What do you mean?" Koontz sputtered. "You saw that pan. And you think that wasn't your lighter?"

Perry looked at Koontz with contempt. "They let the cub go," he said carefully, as if talking to a child. "That bear could be anywhere right now. We're not going to find it in the dark."

High in the hostile peaks near Devils Thumb, far above Sean and Jessie's tiny campfire, a small airplane teetered at the edge of an icy cliff. Frigid winds shook the fragile craft, threatening to sweep it into the deep gorge.

Inside the freezing cockpit Jake Barnes hunched over the radio. Cold, hungry, afraid, and alone, he doggedly tried to send an SOS.

"Mayday. Mayday. This is Super Cub Niner Zero Niner Tango," Jake called weakly. "I've crashed about three miles east of Devils Thumb Pass. Mayday. Mayday."

The radio static faded as the red power light grew dim. The battery's going dead, Jake thought grimly.

Moments later the light went out, and there was nothing but dark, empty silence.

"Damn!" Jake raged, flinging the mike aside.

Realizing he would be stuck there until someone came to find him, Jake gathered his senses. The first thing he needed was food.

Jake located his emergency kit and looked inside. He found a single energy bar. He unwrapped it quickly, then slowed himself down. This bar is all there is, he reminded himself. Better ration it for the long haul.

Jake took the smallest of bites, then carefully rewrapped the bar and stowed it in his pocket.

As he leaned back, a gust of icy wind blasted through a gaping hole in the plane's side. Jake jammed a seat cushion into the hole to block the chill, but the screaming wind blew right through.

Jake remembered the sleeping bag behind him and painfully turned his bruised body to reach it. A bolt of agony shot from his leg to his ribs as he strained to grab it. Finally his fingers hooked it and he pulled.

The sleeping bag wouldn't budge. It was snagged on something. Jake took a deep breath and yanked hard.

A sharp pain stabbed his leg. He kicked out, catching the remaining cabin door. It suddenly dropped open like a trapdoor on a hangman's gallows.

Gasping with terror, Jake clutched his seat as debris around him fell out of the cockpit into the bottomless dark. He could hear it all skittering down the steep mountainside. Then the empty silence closed in.

Heart booming, Jake stared down at the frigid

blackness and gulped. Very carefully he reached over with one hand and pulled the door shut.

Tugging the sleeping bag gingerly, Jake pulled it over his aching body. Never give up, he told himself, but his situation was starting to seem hopeless.

Unable to sleep, he lay in the howling darkness as his damaged plane rocked on the edge of oblivion.

CHAPTER 13

The looming cliffs on either side of the gorge blocked out the sun, so it was always twilight on the water far below. The lack of sunlight also kept the immense ice floes from melting. Jessie and Sean maneuvered the tiny kayak past the jagged blue shards of glacial ice as they pushed deeper into the Alaskan wilderness.

Sean marveled at nature's awesome display of power. Up ahead, Jessie focused on keeping track of their progress. If she had figured correctly, they should be reaching Coogans Pass very soon.

The kayak rounded a bend, and Jessie caught her breath. Both she and her brother stopped paddling and stared at the magnificent snow-coated summit saddled between two rocky peaks straight ahead. The huge mountains rose out of the water and lifted higher than the clouds.

The only way to keep moving was to go around it, over it, or through it. Thankful that they had made it this far, Jessie checked her map. "That's Coogans Pass," she announced. "Let's park it."

"Can I stay in the car?" Sean asked innocently.

Jessie smiled. She was used to her brother's cornball sense of humor. Both of them paddled toward shore and pulled the kayak up on a low area. About twenty yards away, the mouth of a small river emptied into the sea. From her map Jessie knew the river wound back up along a steep gorge through a maze of rocky peaks and glaciers.

Sean peered up at the massive summit blocking their path. "Now what?"

"We climb," Jessie said, unpacking the kayak.

"Up that thing?"

Jessie checked her map. "Dad had to fly this way to get to Devils Thumb—right?"

Sean nodded.

"Then this is the way we have to go."

The two teens shouldered their packs, leaving the kayak beached on the sand, and slowly began hiking up toward the pass.

Jessie and Sean trekked for hours across the unspoiled wilderness, heading out of the timber into a barren region of ice and rock. Huge and terrible mountains jutted up into the dark clouds above them as they climbed.

Less than a mile behind them a baby polar bear climbed awkwardly onto the ridge and scurried after them.

Crazy kids, Sergeant Grazer thought, as he made his tenth phone call in an hour. Bad enough their father's plane had gone missing. Now he had two lost kids and a stolen kayak on top of it. Not to mention Jake's partner, Charlie, who'd been on his case all morning.

Sergeant Grazer was hunched over the phone, but he could feel Charlie staring at him. "Roger that, Elmendorf," he said, loud enough for Charlie to hear. "Be advised we also got two kids missing, possibly in a kayak, heading up the coast. I'd be obliged if you'd keep an eye out for 'em. . . . Okeydoke. Thanks."

Grazer looked up at Charlie. The bush pilot's weathered face was creased with worry.

"The Search-and-Rescue plane has been out twice. They haven't seen any sign of Jake's plane or of the kids."

"But they'll keep looking—right?" Charlie demanded.

Sergeant Grazer turned away. "It's a long shot," he said quietly.

Charlie stood up and snatched his flight jacket from the chair. "Sean and Jessie couldn't have gone far in twenty-four hours," he muttered.

Grazer shook his head. He knew what Charlie was going to do, but he couldn't stop the pilot. "Do you know which way they went?" he challenged.

Charlie grinned as he zipped up his jacket. "Nope. But I've got a pretty good idea."

Just what I need—another hero, Sergeant Grazer thought unhappily, watching Charlie march out of the office. If this keeps up, pretty soon the whole town will be missing.

Mrs. Ben was the only person who saw Charlie's helicopter lift off and roar out over the water toward the distant mountains. Her husband, Ben, and her grandson were out there as well, on their ritual hunt. Shielding her ancient eyes from the sun, Mrs. Ben watched the helicopter skim over the islands.

As she stared at the fading chopper, she uttered a silent prayer, asking for safe return of those she knew and loved.

As she and her brother trudged higher up the mountain, Jessie noticed a snowy ridge above them. That might be a shortcut, Jessie reflected. She looked at Sean, but her brother was lost in his own thoughts. In fact he was even talking to himself.

"What I would give right now to be at a Cubs game," Sean said breathlessly as he climbed. "I can almost smell the fresh-cut grass and the foot-long hot dog just out of the wrapper."

"What's the big deal?" Jessie scoffed. "Baseball's only a game."

Sean stopped, annoyed by the sacrilege. "And this is only a big stinking slab of muddy ice called Alaska." He started climbing faster, fueled by resentment. "By the time I get to see another Cubs game I'll have gray hair and a cane."

"You think by then they'll have won the pennant?" Jessie grinned, tickled by her joke.

Scowling, Sean marched past her. Suddenly a chunk of snow plopped directly onto his head.

"Hey!" Sean whirled and glared at Jessie. "What the—"

"What the what?" Jessie said indignantly. "I didn't do anything."

Sean picked up some snow. Before he could throw it—*splat!* Another chunk of snow smacked the top of Sean's head. They both looked up at the snow-crowned ridge above them. Nothing moved.

Then a shiny black nose appeared as the young polar bear lowered his white head.

"Oh, no," Sean groaned, recognizing the cub. He fingered the lighter in his pocket and remembered Perry's warning. The bear leaned out over the ledge as if teasing Sean.

Jessie smiled. "See? She heard you were a Cubs fan."

"Not that kind of cub." He threw his snowball at the bear. "You dumb animal."

The snowball missed, but the bear ducked out of sight. A long moment later—*phwomp!* A huge shower of snow landed right on Sean.

Jessie burst out laughing. "I think that means 'chill out.' "

Sean gave his sister a look of disgust and continued hiking up the slope. Jessie followed, glancing back every few minutes to check on their new trail mate. Sure enough, the young bear was lumbering along behind them.

"What do you think he wants from us?" Sean said, pausing to look back.

Jessie turned. The bear had also stopped and was watching them. "She probably wants more food," Jessie said sadly.

"Yeah." Sean snorted. "He probably thinks you're lunch. Check out the way he's looking at us. He's hoping we'll fatten him up on macaroni and marshmallow pies. Then as soon as one of us drops"—Sean gave his sister a nasty grin—"it's snack time."

Jessie shuddered and followed her brother higher up the steep, ice-crusted slope. Even though she knew Sean was trying to scare her, Jessie couldn't help wondering why the wild bear was stalking them—and what would happen if it decided to attack.

CHAPTER 14

The motor-powered Zodiac was less mobile than a kayak, especially moving through the maze of ice floes clogging the waters below Coogans Pass.

Koontz navigated carefully, mindful of Perry, who sat in the bow, barking instructions. Although Koontz didn't like Perry, he liked the money they made together. But this search for a missing bear cub was a little crazy.

He slipped the Zodiac between two ice floes, and suddenly two cloud-covered summits loomed dead ahead—between them was Coogans Pass. Perry glanced at Koontz and pointed triumphantly at the shore. At first Koontz didn't understand, but as they neared land, he saw it: pulled up on shore was the kids' kayak.

It didn't take long for Perry and Koontz to pick up Sean and Jessie's trail. The signs were fresh and easy to read—two sets of human footprints leading up the icy incline. And one set of bear tracks. Perry squinted up the mountainside. Koontz pulled out his binoculars and scanned the rugged slope.

"No sign of 'em up there," Koontz muttered. He jabbed his finger at the footprints. "But those are their tracks all right. And that bear's following 'em."

Perry nodded and looked around. "Let's get rid of this kayak before it invites unwanted company."

Koontz didn't really understand, but he dragged the kayak farther inland, then swung it over his head and carried it into the woods. He roughly dumped the kayak out of sight and covered it with dead branches. As he walked back to rejoin Perry he heard it coming—the familiar *thwup-thwup-thwup* of an approaching chopper.

Koontz glanced at Perry. "What's that?"

"Unwanted company," Perry said, squinting into the sky. "Give me one of those paddles."

Koontz didn't get it, but he hefted one of the finely crafted wooden paddles and tossed it to Perry. The hunter caught it with one hand and deftly broke it in half over a rock. He chucked one end of the paddle back to Koontz and pointed at the trees.

Finally Koontz understood. He went back to the kayak's hiding place and buried the broken paddle under the branches.

Before Koontz was finished, an A-Star helicopter roared into view. The chopper blew up a spray of foam as it skimmed the water and landed on the beach.

I hid the kayak just in time, Koontz thought.

Perry waved as the pilot cut the engine and stepped out of the chopper.

As the pilot approached Perry, Koontz came out of the trees, zipping his fly.

"Howdy," the chopper pilot said, his lined face creased in a smile.

"Mornin'," Koontz grunted. "How goes it?"

"Well, not so good." The pilot took the photograph from his pocket. "I'm looking for my partner's kids, a boy and a girl, who may have headed out this way." He handed the photo to Perry. "Their dad's plane went down a couple nights ago," the pilot explained, "and I think they went looking for him."

"Alone?" Perry asked gravely.

The pilot nodded. "I'm afraid so. Have you seen anyone?"

Perry shook his head. "These young people." He sighed. "Weaned on cable TV and video games. They've got no knowledge, no respect for the real brutality of nature."

He sounded so sincere that Koontz almost believed it himself.

"Yeah, right," the pilot said. "What are you guys doing up here?"

Perry was ready for that one. "We're with the Sierra Club."

To Koontz's relief the lie worked.

The chopper pilot grinned and nodded. "Tree-huggers, eh?"

"That's us." Perry chuckled good-naturedly. "We're working on next year's calendar."

The pilot seemed fascinated by the idea. "No kidding."

Perry snapped his fingers. "Say, those two kids, they weren't traveling by kayak, were they?"

The pilot's smile faded. "I think so, why?"

"Oh, dear God . . ."

Perry went to the Zodiac and picked up the broken paddle. "Some poor souls wrecked their kayak on the rocks about twenty-five miles up the coast, one of those native boats. We couldn't get close to the wreckage, but we pulled this out of the water."

Solemnly he handed the paddle to the chopper pilot. The pilot examined it closely, running his fingers over the hand-carved wood. When he looked up at Perry, his face was drained of life.

"Was it theirs?" Perry asked quietly.

"Yeah," the pilot croaked, his throat dry.

"I'm sorry to hear it."

Overcome by emotion, the pilot moved toward his chopper. "Twenty-five miles north of here?" he asked hoarsely.

Perry nodded, his brow knotted with sympathy. "Could be a little farther," he added.

As Koontz watched the helicopter slowly rise and circle north, he had to admire Perry's acting ability. But it was a dirty trick. Perry had signed the kids' death warrant. They'd never survive alone.

The higher Sean and Jessie climbed, the colder it became. The winds were also stronger and cut through their light clothing. Jessie was getting tired, but she was too stubborn to let her brother know that. Amazingly Sean had stopped complaining and was actually being helpful. A few times on the trail he had shown real courage. Jessie was proud of him, but she would never let her brother know that.

The bear continued to amble on behind them, unaffected by the pace, the altitude, or the lack of food. Maybe he had eaten during those few times when he was out of sight, Jessie thought. Or maybe her brother was right about the beast stalking them because it wanted to eat them for dinner. But if that was so, the bear would have made a move by now, she decided. Anyway the cub was really kind of cute. Maybe she could tame it.

She pushed on to keep up with Sean and saw him slowly climbing to the top of the pass. The high altitude made it hard to breathe as she struggled to join him at the summit.

Standing on the airy mountaintop, gazing at the stark peaks around them and the violent water below, Jessie felt a bit dizzy. She took a few deep breaths and pulled the binoculars out of her backpack. It took her less than thirty seconds to pick out the high, narrow mountain with its sharp peak towering above the others.

"Look, Sean, there it is," Jessie said breathlessly, handing him the glasses.

He peered through the binoculars and spotted it way off in the distance. He could see how it had gotten its name. The sharp white peak looked like a long fingernail pointing at the sky. It also appeared to be a thousand miles away.

"Devils Thumb," he said, adjusting the focus.

Jessie nodded. "See anything?"

"Afraid not. We're too far away." He returned the glasses and stared at the long drop to the valley below. A wall of ice almost straight down. "How are we going to get off this pass?" Sean asked calmly. "That's a pretty steep drop."

Jessie reached into her pack. "You want the crampons or the ice ax?"

Sean stared down at the climbing rope, the short ice ax, and the spiked crampons Jessie had brought along. "I'll be the ax man," he said, knowing the crampons were safer.

Jessie gave him a lopsided grin. "All right, ax man. I'll go down about a hundred feet and anchor the rope. Then you follow me. If you slip, you can stop yourself with the ax."

Sean studied the steep decline, then glanced at his sister. "You sure this is how mountain climbers do it?" he asked skeptically.

"That's how they do it on ESPN," Jessie assured him.

Sean shrugged. "Then it must be right." But he was far from convinced. He watched as she put the spiked crampons over her boots and secured the rope.

When she was ready, Jessie took a deep breath and gave the rope to Sean to let out. "Belay me," she instructed him. Then, seeing his confusion, she added, "Hold the rope if I fall."

Sean nodded and gripped the rope with his cold-numbed fingers. Nervously he watched Jessie climb down, her spiked crampons biting into the ice. He slowly played out the rope, his feet braced, ready to break Jessie's fall if she slipped—and if he was strong enough, Sean thought, trying not to look down the almost vertical drop. He looked over the edge as Jessie reached the end of the rope. She stamped out a small platform in the snow, secured the rope around her shoulder, and braced herself to bring Sean down.

A high wind whipped at her hair, and she had to shout to be heard. "Hey, ax man! Your turn!"

As Sean swung one foot over the edge he glanced back and saw the bear a few feet away, watching him intently.

"What're you looking at?" Sean growled, no longer worried about the curious beast.

The polar bear shook his head in disapproval, or so it seemed to Sean. "Oh?" Sean snapped. "And you have a better way?"

Without hesitation the young bear dived headfirst over the ridge. Using his claws as crampons, the bear slid swiftly down the icy slope past a startled Jessie, until he rolled to his feet at the bottom of the cliff.

Mouth open, Sean leaned over and saw the bear straighten up and shake his coat off like a wet dog who'd just come in from the rain. No problem.

"Show-off!" Sean yelled.

Leaning out over the cliff turned out to be a bad mistake. He leaned too far and lost his balance. One foot shot out from under him, and he tumbled head over heels down the deadly drop.

"Sean!" Even as Jessie yelled, her brother slid past her, head down and arms waving wildly. Jessie dug in and frantically pulled on the rope, bracing herself to stop Sean's death tumble.

Suddenly the rope snapped tight, stretched out, then—*thwang!*—yanked Jessie into midair!

Roped together, Jessie and Sean bounced and rolled

down the dizzying incline, sliding faster and faster.
Jessie hit bottom first, her fall cushioned by a snowbank, but Sean wasn't so lucky. When Jessie hit, the
rope swung Sean's weight with lethal speed. Unable
to stop or slow down, he saw only a black blur.

Then his skull smacked into a rock, and the world
shattered like a glass bottle.

CHAPTER 15

The northern lights rippled like a neon rainbow across the sky. On the frozen wasteland below, Sean struggled against the harsh wind and slippery footing, a tiny figure in an immense wilderness of ice, moving toward a dark horizon. Sean felt lost, lonely, and afraid as he pushed into the biting wind. Legs numb, Sean stopped to get his breath. Suddenly he felt something behind him.

He turned and saw the polar bear standing erect in the strange glowing light. Dropping down on all fours the bear slowly moved in another direction, then stopped and looked back.

Sean was dimly aware that the bear wanted him to follow. He tried to walk, but his legs were rigid with exhaustion. The bear took a few more steps, then stopped and looked back.

Unable to move, Sean watched helplessly as the

bear slowly lumbered off toward the distant mountains. A bitter gust of wind whipped along the plain, stirring up clouds of snow. The spindrift veiled the beast from view until it disappeared. All Sean could see was a vibrant white curtain.

Numbly Sean understood that he, too, was fading—dissolving like sugar in a huge white ocean of warm water.

The brightness flickered like the screen of a broken TV.

As Sean fought past the white-hot agony, his eyes fluttered open. Something warm and wet was lapping at his face. For a moment he felt as if he were floating in tropical water.

Smothered by the warm waves, Sean couldn't catch his breath. He opened his eyes one last time and saw huge, savage jaws closing over him.

"Auuuugggghh!" Sean moaned.

Then the blackness swallowed everything. . . .

The polar bear continued to lick Sean's face, but as Jessie stumbled to her brother's side, the bear backed away. Jessie dropped to her knees.

"Are you okay? Sean? *Sean!*" Heart racing with fear, Jessie tried shaking her brother, then rubbed his face with snow.

Sean's eyelids twitched, then opened.

"Sean? Are you okay?"

He groaned with pain and rolled over. "Yes. Could you scream a little louder? I can still hear on this side."

Jessie glanced at the bear. "I thought she was going to—"

"What? Take a bite out of me?"

Jessie nodded.

Sean struggled to sit up. "It's not a *she* anyway. Its a *he*, believe me," he said disgustedly. "I got a good look."

Jessie got up and helped Sean. Her brother took a deep breath and forced himself onto his feet. But he was still half delirious as he surveyed the valley below. Fumbling through his pockets, Sean finally found his compass.

"It's all downhill, isn't it?" he murmured, staring at the compass needle. Suddenly he stumbled forward.

Jessie reached out and caught him before he fell again. Bracing herself, she propped Sean up. Slowly, they began hiking down the mountain, huddled together like Siamese twins.

Sean was still woozy, and Jessie had to help her brother every step of the way. By the time they reached the timberline, Jessie was flustered, worried, and totally exhausted.

They came to a small stream, but as Jessie guided Sean across, she could feel him shivering violently.

"Oh, please, Sean . . . keep going," Jessie mumbled, fighting to keep her balance. When they finally reached the other side, her feet were freezing.

"We have to stop somewhere . . . build a fire," she said breathlessly. "Get you into a sleeping bag."

"No. I'm fine," Sean protested. But his voice shook.

"Yeah. Right," Jessie grunted. "Have you ever heard the expression *hypothermia?*"

"I don't want to stop."

Jessie understood. Until they found someplace to

build a fire they had to keep moving—or freeze to death.

It was becoming painfully clear, though, that unless they found shelter soon, they wouldn't survive more than a few hours. A harsh, frigid wind was whipping through the valley, and the sky was getting dark.

Jessie pushed the fear from her mind and half carried Sean up through a dense tangle of dead bushes and black trees.

"Never give up," Jessie muttered, but her strength was fading fast. As she struggled to reach the crest of a small ridge, Jessie looked around for a decent campsite.

They paused at the top of the ridge. Jessie's head sagged as she tried to catch her breath. Then she looked up and blinked in stunned disbelief.

There, at the edge of a clearing was a decrepit log cabin rising out of the mist like a witch's house in a grim fairy tale. Except this was real.

"Sean, look!" Jessie shouted weakly. "There it is."

Sean lifted his head and tried to smile. "Good. I told you I—" Before he could finish taking credit, Sean crumpled to the ground.

"Sean!" Jessie screamed, kneeling beside him. She lifted Sean's head, but he was unconscious. His lips were turning blue. Jessie tried to pick him up, but his deadweight was too great. Frantically she scanned the area for signs of life. There was only the barren wilderness. Breath heaving in the frozen silence, Jessie sat down beside Sean. A few feet away, the bear sat watching her as if waiting for orders.

Jessie couldn't focus through her fear. Relax, she

told herself, try to think. A moment later it came to her.

Praying her plan would work, Jessie tore off her backpack and dug out the sleeping bag. She unzipped the sleeping bag and rolled Sean's unconscious body inside. Then she zipped up the bag and began dragging it toward the cabin.

Yard by yard Jessie hauled Sean's lifeless body along the ground. A few feet from the door she paused for a moment and studied the cabin.

The log cabin looked to be a hundred years old. Half of it was built right into the mountain, but the sagging roof seemed very close to collapse.

"Hello?" Jessie called. "Is anybody here?"

She waited a few seconds before approaching. At the entrance Jessie hesitated, listening. Finally she pushed open the door and ducked inside.

It was another world. As Jessie's eyes slowly got used to the dim light, she saw the strange clutter littering the low, dark room. Rows of animal skulls were arranged on the dusty shelves—along with yellowed magazine photos. Up in the dusty rafters someone had stored a pair of skis, as well as snowshoes and other objects, all old and battered.

Jessie was relieved to see a potbellied stove. Hoping it still worked, she went outside. Sean was dozing in the sleeping bag. Gathering her strength, Jessie grabbed the bag and began pulling her brother into the cabin.

The helicopter had been in the air too long, Charlie thought, checking his fuel gauge. The engine was making some odd noises.

He scanned the coastal islands below, then veered back toward Devils Thumb for another look.

"I've been up and down the whole of the inside passage," Charlie reported by radio, "and I haven't seen a thing. I'm gonna head back and refuel."

Sergeant Grazer's voice crackled from the speaker. "Roger, Charlie. You've been out all day. Take a breather."

"Roger that," Charlie muttered wearily.

Charlie banked the chopper into a steep turn and headed for home.

CHAPTER 16

From time to time, as Jessie chopped firewood with a rusty ax, she would check the darkening sky. There was no sign of a search plane.

Jessie carried an armful of wood inside. The potbellied stove was glowing warmly. Jessie set the wood down beside it, then stirred a can of soup heating on the stove. Dinner was almost ready.

Sean sat up in his sleeping bag on the floor near the stove, still groggy.

Jessie took out her crumpled map and went to the open doorway, where the light was better. She studied the map, but it was no use. She knew where they were—but not where they were going. Suddenly a strange rustling sound drew her eyes to the trees nearby. Jessie ducked behind the door and peered at the darkening forest. Then she spotted the bear cub moving through the trees. He slowly lumbered closer and stopped outside the cabin door.

For a long moment the bear and Jessie stared at each other. Then the bear took a step closer.

"Shoo!" Jessie ordered. "No wild bears allowed."

The bear backed off a few steps and sat down, his soft brown eyes looking dejected.

Probably wants another marshmallow pie, Jessie thought. Then she remembered the soup. She went back to the stove and used an old rag to pick up the hot can.

She quickly ate half the soup and gave the rest to her brother. Sean took the can in both hands and gulped down the warm broth.

"Well, we can stay here tonight," Jessie said cheerfully. "At least we have a fire."

Sean tried to get to his feet. "What do you mean 'stay'? There's plenty of daylight left."

Jessie gently pushed him back. "You should lie down," she scolded. "Get a good night's sleep. You're not thinking straight."

Sean pointed at the dusty window. "Dad is out there now. You think *he's* going to get a good night's sleep?"

"I think he'd want *you* to," Jessie said firmly, "after hitting your head like that."

"He's not worrying about me," Sean said. He touched the deep purple bruise over his eye and winced.

Jessie folded her arms. "What am I supposed to tell Dad after you die from exposure?"

Sean began rummaging through his backpack. "Tell him I died trying to find him," he said with mock bravado.

"I'm sure that'll make him feel *real* good, Sean."

Jessie sighed and put another log in the stove. "Look, you have to get some rest. We've got at least two days of walking along the river. And then we still have to climb Devils Thumb."

Sean took a cracker from his pack, bit off a piece, then pointed at the ceiling with a knowing smile. "You can walk if you like, Jessie. I'm taking the canoe."

It took Jessie a few seconds to see it. Perched on the dusty cross beams—along with snowshoes, old wooden skis, rusty pots, and other abandoned junk—was a canvas canoe.

Sean's smile grew wider as he got to his feet. "Where's that ax you found?"

When Jessie fetched the ax, Sean grabbed the handle and began poking it into the rafters, sending down a thick blizzard of dust. Sean's smile faded. He grasped the handle tighter and jumped up, trying to jab the canoe.

Sean missed the canoe but hit the old beam. One end sagged and a huge wave of junk began sliding down on him.

"Seeaaann!" Even before she yelled, Jessie was moving. She shoved Sean aside as the pile of skis, broken radios, pans, tin cups, motor parts, paddles—and the canoe—crashed to the floor like a dust bomb.

A dark gray mushroom cloud filled the room. Choking and coughing, Jessie and Sean rubbed the dust from their eyes.

"Oh, yuk!" Jessie sputtered.

Sean tried to laugh but started coughing again. He crawled over and pulled the canoe from the junk heap littering the floor.

With a proud smirk Sean lifted one end of the canoe like a prize fish. "*Really*, Jessie. I brought the compass. I found the canoe. I mean—where would you be without me?"

Triumphantly, Jessie poked her hand through one of the ragged holes in the canoe's side. "Pretty much where I am now, *Sean*."

Sean's face fell when he saw the holes torn in the canvas. He dropped the canoe and watched Jessie rummaging through her pack.

This time it was Jessie's turn to smirk. She pulled out a roll of duct tape and tossed it to Sean.

Sean immediately tore off a stretch of tape and covered one of the holes. Amazingly, it seemed to patch the canvas.

"I packed it just in case I had to tape your mouth shut," Jessie said. "I hope there's some left for the canoe."

After mending the canoe Jessie and Sean had no problem getting to sleep.

They awoke at dawn. Jessie insisted that Sean share another can of soup. It would probably be their last hot meal for a while.

Sean seemed to have recovered after a good night's rest, but he still had trouble keeping up with Jessie. His sister charged down the valley, pausing only once to check her map.

Jessie was right on target. It was still early morning when they reached a clear mirror lake at the outlet of a small, swift river. At the edge of the lake Jessie and Sean looked at each other then carefully lowered the patched canoe into the cold water.

Like a ragged swan it floated grandly on the mirror surface. Jessie beamed proudly at Sean.

"Look at that. Perfect. Where would you be without me?"

Sean rolled his eyes skyward. "Probably back home in Chicago."

As they began loading their gear into the canoe, Sean noticed the bear cub slowly circling them. The bear hesitated, then edged nearer, as if he wanted to get into the canoe with them.

Sean waved him away. "You're out of luck, Cubby. We're full up."

Jessie looked at the bear, looked at Sean, then got into the canoe. "Cubby?" she repeated. "Where did you get *that* name?"

Sean carefully climbed into the canoe and lifted his paddle. He dipped the paddle into the water and pushed the craft away from shore. As the canoe drifted into deeper water, Sean watched the bear cub make his way along the bank.

"It's what his mother called him," Sean said finally.

Jessie groaned softly and kept paddling as the canoe picked up speed and cruised swiftly toward the foaming river.

CHAPTER 17

Alone inside the wreckage of his plane, Jake Barnes remained wrapped in his sleeping bag. The relentless wind rocked the fuselage, but Jake was too cold and too hungry to sleep. Exhausted, he carefully turned his bruised body, and his eyes fell on the family photo stuck to the dashboard: Dawn, Sean, and Jessie.

"Well, guys," Jake muttered, "what do you say we eat a little dinner?"

The joke was on him. When he opened the energy bar wrapper it was empty. So much for the main course, Jake thought. Maybe some dessert will do.

Jake painfully reached out and scooped up a handful of snow from inside the broken windshield. Just don't swallow any glass, he reminded himself as he chewed the cold snow.

A fluttering sound drew his eye. Jake saw the family photo being lifted by the strong gusts blowing through the window. He lunged for the photo, and the sudden movement shifted the plane's balance. Jake scrambled back, but it was too late.

Slowly, the fuselage toppled over the ledge.

Jake slammed against the ceiling as the plane rolled over and slid down the steep slope. The fuselage thundered over ice and rocks, gathering speed. Inside, Jake's limp body spun and pounded against the metal frame.

The family photo fell from his fingers and vanished in a roaring white swirl of snow. With violent suddenness the tumbling plane wrenched to an abrupt stop.

Jake smacked hard against the door, and it flew open. A blast of frigid air roused his numbed senses, and he opened his eyes.

As Jake's brain began to focus, his stomach turned inside out. He was dangling from the open doorway— staring at a dizzying thousand-foot drop.

Above him he could see that the plane's tail was jammed between two rock outcroppings. The fuselage was hanging above sheer nothingness.

And so was he. Jake didn't dare look again at the terrifying fall of a thousand feet. Instead he searched inside the cockpit for something he could grab.

Jake had somehow managed to hook one arm around the seat, but half of him was still outside, swaying in the wind. Agony lanced through his battered body as he pulled himself up and hugged the seat with his other arm.

Shivering with pain, he heaved himself inside the cockpit. He crawled behind the seat, gasping like a hooked fish.

Trapped inside the wind-whipped craft a thousand feet above the earth, Jake fought back with the only weapon he had.

"Never give up . . . never give . . . never . . ." Jake repeated feverishly. But inside the dangling metal coffin the words had a hollow ring.

Paddling along the clear blue water that curled between breathtaking ice peaks, Jessie was awed by nature's raw beauty. She felt small and insignificant as they passed massive glaciers shimmering in the sun like huge diamonds.

Sean and Jessie had no problem guiding the canoe downstream in the rapid water. Jessie occasionally looked back and saw Cubby padding along the riverbank. The young bear had managed to keep up with the canoe, even swimming for short stretches.

Jessie's eyes drifted to her brother, who was wearing an intent frown.

Riding behind his sister, Sean kept remembering the last words he had exchanged with his father: "I wish you had died instead of Mom."

They had to find him, Sean told himself. Never give up. Never give up. Just like Cubby. The young bear had stayed with them mile after mile. Cubby scrambled over rocks, swam across rough water, overcoming all obstacles to keep up. "Look at him," Sean said with an amazed grin. "He's relentless."

Jessie smiled sadly at the young bear struggling to keep up with them. "We're the only family he has now."

A few miles farther downstream Cubby was actually twenty or thirty yards ahead of the canoe when he stopped short. The young bear leaned over the edge of a steep rock and sniffed the air. Suddenly one of his rear paws slipped.

Cubby's big front paws gripped the rock, halting his slide. Footing secure, the young bear lifted his head. His pink ears twitched and he stood up, as if listening hard.

Cubby looked back at the approaching canoe and made a worried *whuff* sound.

Jessie glanced up in time to see Cubby dive off the steep rock and begin swimming toward their canoe. She looked at Sean, who shrugged.

"What now, Cubby?" Sean called out.

The silence that followed was filled with a faint rumble, like a distant train. Jessie heard it, too. The rumble came closer, rising to an ominous roar.

"Uh, oh," Jessie muttered, digging her paddle into the water. Her heart dropped as the canoe came around the bend.

They were racing directly into a boiling rush of industrial-strength rapids. The wildly foaming water was choked with sharp rocks, haystack waves, whirling chutes, and bottomless holes. The churning mass was officially known as class four white water. Class five was the red storm on Jupiter.

"Paddle for shore!" Sean yelled.

Jessie dipped her paddle and Sean did the same, leaning against the waves. The current shot the light canoe toward a rock ledge, but Jessie saw it coming. "Brace! Brace!" she shouted. "Backpaddle. Left! Left!"

Jessie reached out and jammed the paddle into the foaming water, bracing the canoe. Sean did the same, and the craft veered sharply, just missing a rock.

The canoe hit a swift current and shot forward, bobbing and weaving on the choppy water as it swiftly skidded downstream. Furiously working her paddle, Jessie guided the craft through treacherous whirlpools, barking out orders. "Forward now! Hard!"

Swept onward by the raging current, the canoe plunged into a haystack. The surging water lifted the craft like a twig, flinging it high in the air as the wave crested, then broke.

The canoe plunged and hit the water with a jarring *phwomp!* Jessie worked her paddle, and the craft slid between two mean-looking rocks and glided into the calmer swirls downstream.

Jessie smiled in disbelief. "We made it?"

Sean grinned. "We made it, Jessie!"

Slowly Jessie's smile spread wider. They looked at each other, savoring the moment.

"You did it!" Sean congratulated her.

"We did it," Jessie said modestly.

They kept grinning at each other, brother and sister united. Suddenly Jessie saw Sean's grin crumble. His gaze was fixed up ahead. When Jessie turned, her heart jumped into her throat.

Directly ahead was the end of the world. And the raging river was pouring over the edge—taking them with it.

A ghostly mist swirled above the thundering waterfall, as if the bottom had dropped out of the river.

Sean and Jessie jammed their paddles hard, but it was far too late. They were going over.

"Oh, no! Come on!" Jessie screamed. "We gotta go for it! *Forward hard now!*"

Her screams were lost in the howling water as the canoe plunged over the falls and vanished in the seething mist.

CHAPTER 18

For an endless moment the canoe seemed to float on the thundering mist. Then with breathtaking speed it dropped into a foaming hole at the bottom of the waterfall.

Long seconds, then minutes passed. Then suddenly, about twenty yards downstream, Sean's head popped out of the water. Seconds later Jessie came up, sputtering and coughing up water. Gasping for breath, Sean swam to his sister's side and motioned for her to follow him.

Exhausted, he tried vainly to swim to shore against the powerful current sweeping them downstream. As Sean crested over a cascading wave he glimpsed a fallen tree. Its limbs hung over the rushing water directly ahead.

Sean used his remaining strength to swim to the tree. As he hurtled closer, Sean reached up desperately and hooked it. Holding on with everything he had left, he looked around for his sister.

Instantly he saw Jessie coming toward him—then rushing past. He reached out blindly and grasped her arm.

"Hang on!" he croaked. "Climb up onto the tree!"

Squeezing tight he lifted Jessie out of the water until she could grab a tree branch and climb onto the trunk.

As soon as Jessie got her balance, she reached down for Sean, who was still clinging to a branch in the violent water. When her fingers closed around his, Jessie heard a crack. Sean's branch snapped, and his hand jerked free.

In disbelief she watched Sean being swept downstream by the thundering current.

"Sean!" Jessie screamed. "Seeeeaaaaan!"

But her screams were muffled by the river's roar as her brother disappeared around a bend.

Tumbling and twisting in the savage torrent Sean gulped for air and swallowed water. Gagging, he sank underwater and was pushed up again by the raging current.

Helplessly Sean flailed his tired arms against the sheer walls of the gorge. Suddenly a wave threw him against a rock outcropping.

Sean grabbed hold of the boulder as the current pressed him against it. Breathing heavily, he tried to claw his way up onto the slippery rock, but his tired fingers couldn't keep a grip.

Slowly he slid back into the violent water until a

gnarled hand came out of nowhere. In one smooth motion the hand grabbed Sean under the arm and lifted him onto the rock.

Breathless, gazed, and blinded by the bright sun, Sean squinted up at his rescuer—a dark figure wearing a hood.

As if in a dream, the figure pulled back his hood and bent closer. It took Sean a numbed moment before he recognized Ben. The old man's wrinkled face broke into a wide grin.

Gasping in stunned disbelief, Sean lay there looking up at Ben. Then another face leaned into view. Sean blinked, sure it couldn't be true.

It was Jessie's friend Chip!

"Hey, Sean," Chip said cheerfully, as if nothing had happened. "What are you doing here?"

The native hunting camp included two tents. A big freight canoe with an outboard motor was piled up on the riverbank next to a pile of hunting gear.

Sean and Jessie, wrapped in blankets, sat around the campfire. Chip was crouched beside them.

Ben and Chip's father, John Wood, appeared on the riverbank. Ben was carrying something. As the two men neared the fire Sean noticed they were soaking wet from the waist down.

Ben tossed Jessie's drenched backpack onto the ground. "We saved some of your gear, but your canoe is history."

"You guys are an awful long way from home," Mr. Wood grumbled, moving closer to the fire. "You say they couldn't find your father—with planes and helicopters?"

"They were looking in the wrong place," Sean said stubbornly.

Mr. Wood shook his head in disbelief. "And you were expecting to find him on foot?"

"I'm sorry to hear Jake's missing," Mr. Wood said quietly. "But whatever happened to his plane, you two going up there alone isn't going to help him. I'll take you back to town tomorrow in the boat."

"No," Sean said with cold certainty. "We can't go back."

Mr. Wood sighed. "And I can't be responsible for your deaths," he said flatly. "What do you want me to tell—"

"Tell them we never stopped looking for our father," Jessie declared.

Sean looked at Jessie gratefully.

Chip's father squinted unhappily. "You kids have no appreciation for this country," he told them sternly. "Nothing you've seen so far will test you like what you'll find up there, on Devils Thumb."

"That's why they need to go," Ben put in solemnly.

Mr. Wood rolled his eyes.

Ben came closer and pointed at his son, eyes blazing in the firelight. "You listen to me, young man," he said with sudden authority. "We've gone to great pains to create a ritual for Chip, to make him a man, like we did for you twenty years ago."

Chip's father crossed his arms and nodded.

Ben peered at the others. His craggy face resembled a totem mask as he moved in front of the dancing flames. "In my father's time a young man had to hunt a bear with only a spear in his hand, and so took on the bear's power—or died trying."

Ben looked over at Mr. Wood. "Only now we go on hunting trips mostly to get out of town for a couple of days, and get away from our wives," he said with disgust.

Embarrassed, Chip rolled his eyes at Jessie. She gave him a quick smile. When she looked back, she saw Ben staring at her intently as if he could see inside her. "But these two," Ben went on solemnly, "are on a true journey. A spirit journey. They've come too far. It'd be wrong to stop them now."

John Wood sighed and looked crosswise at his father.

"Are you finished, Dad?" he asked quietly.

Ben folded his arms. "Yes."

John looked over at Sean and Jessie. "Their spirit journey is at an end," he said carefully. "This is the nineties, old man. We'll head home first thing in the morning."

Without waiting for an answer, he left the campfire. Ben shrugged and joined the others, who sat in dejected silence.

Sean and Jessie exchanged a glance. Ben was right— they had come too far to stop now.

Later that night Sean sat alone at the edge of camp, staring up at Devils Thumb, its sharp peak outlined by the northern lights.

The rippling neon colors were only a small part of the magnificent light show. The sky blazed with the fire of a billion stars in their magnificent universal dance.

Sitting on a rock, wrapped in an Eskimo parka, Sean chewed on caribou meat as he contemplated the sky. As he raised a chunk of meat to his lips, he heard a rustle in the darkness. He kept very quiet as he turned slightly toward the sound. A familiar shape came out of the shadows. Cubby stood a few yards away, his eyes gleaming in the dim light. He looked at Sean, then gazed off in the direction of Devils Thumb.

Sean slowly stood up and held out a piece of meat. The young bear hesitated.

Carefully, Sean inched closer, his hand extended.

Cubby lowered his head and sniffed at the meat. Holding his breath, Sean took a small step nearer.

The bear stretched out his neck and took the food from Sean's hand.

At that moment Sean knew his life had changed forever.

Just before dawn the entire world seemed to be asleep.

Sean and Jessie were bunked in Ben's tent, but there was no sign of the old man. Both Jessie and Sean were in deep slumber until a high zipping sound woke Jessie.

She sat up and saw Chip's head poke through the unzipped tent flap. Chip glanced around to make sure the coast was clear, then grinned at Jessie.

"Hi," he whispered.

Jessie got up stiffly. "Hi."

Sean lifted his head and blinked at Chip.

Chip's grin faded. "My dad says he's going to get

the two of you home safely if he has to tie you to the boat," he said.

Jessie glanced at Sean. Her brother didn't speak, but he looked ready to stand his ground and fight.

Chip saw it, too. He motioned for them to follow him. "So hurry up," he whispered. "We have to get you out of here before my dad wakes up."

Still groggy, Jessie and Sean followed him outside. The sun was about to peek over the horizon as Chip led them to the outskirts of the camp. Jessie's newly dried backpack was there waiting for them.

Chip handed the backpack to Jessie. "I packed some food and stuff for you guys—caribou jerky."

Jessie took the backpack and smiled at Chip. "Your dad's going to kill you."

Chip shrugged. "Then you can come to my funeral. Don't be late."

"Thanks," Jessie murmured, searching for the right words. "This is very . . . manly of you."

She bent closer and kissed him on the cheek. Blushing, Chip gave her a huge grin.

Then a voice came from the darkness: "There's a white bear over there staring at you."

Chip, Jessie, and Sean were all startled to see Ben standing beside them.

The old man smiled. He fixed his eyes on Sean and pointed upward. Like a gray-white ghost, Cubby appeared out of the shadows and stood on a rocky ledge just above them.

Jessie felt a rush of relief. "Cubby! He made it!"

Cubby hopped off the rock and ran over to playfully lick Jessie's hands and face.

"He's been following us since the day before yesterday," Sean explained to Chip and Ben.

Jessie gently rubbed the bear's head. "His mother was killed by poachers."

Ben looked at the bear, then at Sean and Jessie. "This sort of thing doesn't happen every day, you know," he said gruffly. "I'd say he's looking out for you two."

Sean snorted. "He's 'looking out' for more food. He had dinner with us a couple of nights."

The old man smiled sadly as if disappointed.

"Some things, Sean, you can see only by opening your heart."

The quiet words touched something inside Sean. He looked at Ben and nodded. Then Sean grinned. "Or by opening a box of marshmallow pies."

Ben laughed. He shuffled closer to the bear, then squatted down beside him.

Ben and Cubby seemed to be deep in conversation as the old man gently rubbed the bear's head. Ben was chanting something in his native language, which ended with the word *"Nanook."*

Then he turned to Sean and Jessie. "In the old days we called the polar bear 'one who gives power,' " Ben explained gravely. "To touch him is a gift. Don't throw it away."

The old man reached out and clasped Sean's hand. Slightly spooked, Sean pulled back. When he glanced down at his hand, his eyes went wide. There was something in his fist.

Sean slowly unfolded his fingers, revealing a bear carved in wood. The figurine hung from a rawhide thong. Sean looked at Ben, who just smiled. Unable

117

to speak, Sean hung the figurine around his neck and gave Ben the V sign. Then he followed Jessie and Cubby, who were already trudging toward Devils Thumb.

" 'Bye," Chip called softly. But his words were lost in the wind.

CHAPTER 19

From the air the coastal wilderness seemed to be endless. Charlie eased the chopper down lower and squinted through the dawn mists rising from the water. He flipped on the radio and picked up the mike.

"Quincy, come in."

"Quincy here, over."

Charlie recognized Sergeant Grazer's voice. But as he started to answer, something caught his attention.

"Hold it," Charlie said, pulling the chopper around. "I think I found something."

Cruising lower, Charlie saw some equipment and what seemed to be the remains of a campfire near a sandy cove.

He peered out the window, the mike still pressed against his mouth. "It's some sort of camp," he reported. "I'm gonna go in low to take a look. The place is a mess."

"Is it a kid's mess?" Grazer asked hopefully.

Charlie swung the chopper around, skimming the treetops. "Nope," he muttered, spotting the concealed tents and fuel tanks below. "I'm gonna set her down."

Skillfully, Charlie landed on a small section of open beach a few yards from the camp. He hopped out of the chopper and slowly approached the site.

The camp was deserted, but there were signs of recent activity everywhere. Charlie looked inside one tent, and his eyes widened. The tent was stuffed with piles of animal furs.

Slowly Charlie's brain shifted into gear. He took in the fuel tanks and supply tent hidden under netting. Then he examined the piles of skins.

"Poachers," he grunted under his breath. But there was something more. The whole setup seemed familiar, as if he'd visited before. Then he spotted an inflatable raft pulled up on shore and half concealed under some branches—a Zodiac.

Suddenly Charlie remembered where he'd seen the Zodiac.

The phony Sierra Club explorers—the ones who had claimed the kids were lost. Charlie's jumbled thoughts suddenly clicked into place.

Without hesitating, he ran back to the chopper and grabbed the mike. "Sergeant Grazer, you'd better send somebody out here pronto. Those guys I ran into were poachers. They sent me on a wild-goose chase," Charlie added grimly. "I'm heading back up toward Devils Thumb."

Less than three minutes later the chopper was high in the air, banking toward the distant peaks.

*　　*　　*

When Sean finally reached the ridge below Devils Thumb, Cubby was waiting for him. Smiling, Sean glanced back at his sister. Then his face clouded.

Jessie was struggling to climb up, but the fierce wind made it difficult. Sean reached down and hauled her onto the crest.

Breathless, Jessie collapsed against a rock. After a moment's rest she rummaged through her pack and pulled out the well-worn map.

She studied the map, then looked at Sean. "Dad went up that way," she declared, raising her voice in the high wind. "If we follow this ridge—"

As Jessie pointed up to her right, a sharp gust of wind tore the map from her fingers. Helplessly she watched it flutter down the mountainside like a large snowflake and disappear.

"Sean. The map!" she wailed.

He shrugged. "Never mind. We have to keep going northeast—that way."

"Sean, you wouldn't know the difference between north and south without a comp—" Jessie's mouth dropped open when she saw the brand-new Silva Compass dangling by its cord from Sean's hand. "You had that all along?"

"Of course." Sean smiled smugly. "How do you think we got *this* far?" He made a big show of checking the needle to find their bearings.

Jessie felt like smacking him. Instead she did the next best thing. " 'A *compass*, Dad?' " she whined. " 'Duh, what'm I supposed to do with a *compass?* ' "

Sean gave her a long, hard look. Then he held out his hand and helped her hike up to where Cubby was waiting.

The wind blew stronger and colder as Sean and Jessie climbed higher. They would be all right as long as they kept moving, Sean thought. But it might get bad after the sun set.

They reached a large ledge jutting out between Devils Thumb and a huge glacier. Sean looked up to his right and scanned the sharp peak for any sign of his father's plane.

Then he turned and studied the glacier. The icy face dropped down to their left. More ice rose up into another pass.

"That's Devils Thumb Pass!" Jessie yelled, pointing to their right.

Sean nodded and headed into the teeth of the wind. When he looked back, he noticed that Cubby was lumbering in the opposite direction toward the other pass.

"Where does he think he's going?" Sean asked no one in particular. He paused and watched the young bear continue toward the glacial pass.

"Hey!" Jessie called out, a bit scared. First she'd lost the map; now they were losing Cubby.

The bear glanced back over his shoulder. His gleaming brown eyes seemed to stare directly at Sean.

"I think he wants us to follow him," Sean said.

"No!" Jessie shouted. "Dad wouldn't have flown that way."

Sean watched Cubby drop down on all fours and continue toward the glacier. Then the cub stopped, turned, and looked back to see if they were following.

Just like the bear in my dream, Sean thought, somewhat awed. "Maybe Cubby knows something we don't," he said finally.

Jessie was horrified. "Sean, I know Dad's route. I know how far he could have flown," she reminded him. "He has to be somewhere in Devils Thumb Pass. You have to trust me."

As Sean watched Cubby start toward the glacier, he absently touched the carved bear that hung around his neck. "No, Jessie," he said evenly, "you have to trust the bear."

Jessie stared at Sean. She could tell from the set of his jaw that he meant it. She gazed up at Devils Thumb Pass one last time and sighed.

Without a word Sean and Jessie backed down the ridge and headed toward the glacier pass.

Wedged inside his battered plane dangling over the cliff face, Jake Barnes huddled in his sleeping bag. He was pale, weak, and only half conscious.

Thwup-thwup . . . thwup-thwup . . .

The sound of a distant chopper carried clearly in the mountain air. Jake opened his eyes and painfully sat up, listening.

"Hey," Jake croaked. "Hey! Help! Help!"

He fumbled for the flare gun, but the chopper was approaching too quickly. It roared overhead, then went past, floating above him like a sleek gray shark.

Helplessly Jake watched it cruise out of sight. Then the silence closed over him like a door. His body aching, he settled back under the sleeping bag.

Determined to be ready next time, Jake kept his fingers wrapped around the flare gun. But he doubted there would be a next time.

Jake wasn't sure he could survive another night.

*　　　*　　　*

Remembering what happened the last time he followed Cubby, Sean advanced carefully through the icy pass. Sean knew Jessie was exhausted, but they had to keep moving.

Far ahead, the bear stopped and patiently waited for Sean and Jessie to come into view around a curve. Then he got up, shook himself, and continued on.

About a hundred yards farther along the snow-carpeted glacier, Cubby paused and sniffed the wind. The bear's ears pricked up as a faint whine drifted closer.

Sean saw Cubby standing ahead of them and looked around at Jessie.

Suddenly a chopper appeared above the glacier, flying low. As it circled, Sean shaded his eyes, trying to see the pilot.

When Sean spotted Koontz behind the stick, his first reaction was disappointment, closely followed by fear.

Cubby whirled and started running wildly away from the helicopter. The chopper banked sharply, throwing up clouds of snow, and chased after the bear.

At the same time Sean charged forward to help Cubby. In disbelief he watched the hunter, Perry, lean out the chopper's side door and take aim.

"Nooo!" Sean shouted desperately.

But his cry was useless. The shot cracked through the engine's rumble.

Cubby stopped dead in his tracks and collapsed in a furry heap. As Sean came closer, he saw the shiny red stains on Cubby's soft white neck.

Sean heard something and looked back. Jessie was scrambling forward along the glacier, her eyes wide with horror. The chopper swooped low like a dark eagle and hovered beside the fallen bear.

Perry jumped down, scooped Cubby up out of the snow, then rolled the bear's limp body into the helicopter.

The hunter clambered aboard the chopper, then gave Sean and Jessie a smug grin. "Morning, Sean. Jessie," he called out. "Small world, isn't it? Have a nice hike."

As the chopper slowly lifted off, Sean felt Jessie brush him aside.

"No! *Noooo!*" Jessie screamed, staggering up the gentle slope.

Sean and Jessie watched in stunned silence as the helicopter soared higher and disappeared between the peaks. Then Sean turned to Jessie. She was staring up at the empty sky sobbing, tears streaming down her face.

"He's gone, Sean," she wailed. "Those murderers took him away for no reason."

In a sudden surge of anger Jessie grabbed a loose rock and flung it into the sky. "Why did it have to be him?" she cried. "Cubby didn't do anything wrong. It's not fair!"

Jessie's shouts echoed in the cold wind as she slowly sank to the ground. "What do we do now?" she sobbed.

Sean looked up at the pass. Then he grabbed his sister by the shoulders. "We keep going," he told her. "Mom would have wanted us to keep going. 'Never give up,' she would have said. 'Never!' " He pulled Jessie to her feet. "Can't you hear her?"

Jessie shook her head. "But where do we go?"

Sean pointed up the pass. "This way. We keep going where Cubby was taking us." He tugged at his sister's arm. "We have to."

Jessie pulled back. "Sean, I can't climb any more. I'm tired."

Sean looked at the dark blue circles under Jessie's eyes and her pale skin. His sister was running on empty. She'd put up a game fight without complaining, but now she needed his help.

"I know," Sean said gently. "Come on. I'll carry you if I have to."

Jessie felt a warm wave of relief. Charged by her brother's promise, she wiped away her tears. As she started to drag herself along the glacier, Jessie saw something in the snow. When she stepped closer, the sight stunned her like a lightning bolt.

Jessie dropped to her knees and pulled a colored rectangle from the snow. Feverishly she brushed it clean with cold-numbed fingers. It was an old curled-up snapshot. Jessie blinked in disbelief.

It was the family photograph from her father's airplane.

"He's here," Jessie said, her voice cracking. "Dad's here!"

Sean's face lit up when he recognized the snapshot. Without a word the two of them began trudging up the glacier, their renewed hope giving them fresh energy.

CHAPTER 20

The gray chopper made a lazy circle over the pass and headed toward base camp. Perry cradled his rifle, his deep-set blue eyes glowing with victory. Smugly he looked over at the bear cub's still body on the rear seat.

"One way or another, if you're persistent, fortune always smiles on you," Perry gloated.

Koontz revved up the engine, pulled the chopper over a ridge, and dropped between two peaks. "Yahoo!" he yelled. "I love this job."

Perry leaned back and pulled a short tranquilizer dart from the bear's neck. As he started to clean the bloodstain, the cub's eyelids fluttered.

"How much tranquilizer did you put in this dart?" Perry asked with annoyance.

Koontz half turned. "Four cc's. Why?"

The cub's paws moved, and he tried to lift his head.

"Well, it wasn't enough," Perry snapped. "Set her down. I'll have to dart him again."

Koontz scanned the area and spotted a small, flat clearing between the mountains. Landing would be routine, but taking off again might be tricky. He had no choice. With practiced ease he quickly set the chopper down.

As soon as they landed, Perry loaded another drugged dart into his rifle and hopped out for a better shot.

A ball of white-hot pain leaped onto Perry. Clawing, scratching, biting, the young bear savagely attacked his captor. Perry, his face twisted in pain, struggled to fight off the savage beast. He swung back and clubbed the bear with his rifle. At that moment Koontz came running around the chopper with a shotgun.

When Koontz brought his gun up to fire, the cub's teeth clamped down on Perry's knee with viselike power.

"Arrgh," Perry screeched. Crazed with pain, he fired his rifle.

He missed. The dart hit Koontz square in the neck. On reflex Koontz squeezed the trigger, and his shotgun blasted the chopper's instrument panel.

The panel sizzled loudly, then erupted in a volcano of sparks and black smoke.

The bear cub suddenly leaped over Perry, knocking the hunter aside as he bounded up the mountain toward freedom. Grunting with effort, Perry limped after the bear, but the effort was useless.

Perry turned and saw Koontz standing there with a

dumb smile on his face. Slowly, like a tree falling down, the pilot keeled over in the snow.

Dazed, exhausted, and seriously wounded, Perry looked around in shock. His pilot was unconscious, the chopper was badly damaged, and his knee was pounding with agony.

In the space of a few minutes the young bear had gone from captive to conqueror.

High on the mountain now, Sean and Jessie were two black dots on a gleaming white field of ice. They were connected to each other by a worn climbing rope. Sean used it to pull his sister up as the slope became steeper.

There was no trail. All they could do was keep climbing, and it was getting tougher with each step.

Sean spotted a ledge about twenty yards above them and angled over. It would make a good rest stop.

Carefully Sean found some footing and heaved himself onto the ledge. Then he pulled his sister up alongside him.

His breath ragged, Sean searched the mountainside. Then he spotted it. "Look!" Sean cried.

Jessie followed his finger and saw a patch of yellow in the white snow. An airplane wing, Super Cub yellow.

They hurried up the steep hill and found more wreckage: a twisted metal float torn off like paper, large jagged fragments, broken glass.

But no Jake Barnes.

"Dad!" Sean shouted. *"Daaaaad!"*

"Daddy, where are you?" Jessie called, her voice trembling. Her stomach pounded with cold fear.

Nobody could have survived this crash. *"Daaaaaaaaaaaaad!"* she screamed, and heard Sean's voice rising with hers in the howling wind.

Jake Barnes lay completely still beneath the sleeping bag. The sound of Sean's and Jessie's cries came as faint moans through the freezing gusts, distant and dreamlike.

Jake's eyes fluttered open. He squinted in the bright light, listening. Was that Sean's voice? Jake wondered. Probably a feverish hallucination, he decided, closing his eyes.

"Dad . . ."

Jake's eyes opened wide. That was no hallucination. It was Sean's voice. With great effort he tried to sit up, but the pain—and the danger of falling out of the plane—held him back.

"Seaaa—" Jake croaked, his voice cracking with exhaustion. It was no use. No one could hear him.

Then he remembered the flare gun.

Jake turned his head and saw the gun a few inches from his cold, stiff fingers. Fumbling, he grasped the handle and with great difficulty poked the gun through a hole in the plane's wall.

Gasping with effort, he managed to squeeze the trigger. Then his head dropped, and the gun fell from his numb fingers.

A bright red flare shot into the sky, trailed by a thick plume of smoke.

"Sean, look!" Jessie shouted.

Sean turned in time to see the flare arc upward. "Dad's alive!" he yelled, pointing at the deep skid marks in the snow. The marks ended at the edge of a cliff.

Frantically he and Jessie hurried to the cliff and knelt down, peering over the edge.

What was left of the plane was dangling over a dizzying drop two thousand feet above the earth. The Super Cub was barely held in place by the slimmest of threads: the tail section was wedged between two narrow rocks jutting out of the face of the cliff.

Any slight movement, even a stiff breeze, could send their father plummeting to certain doom.

"Hold on, Dad!" Sean called out. "I'm gonna come down there to get you!"

"No, you're not," Jessie muttered, uncoiling the rope. "I'll go down. You can lower me. I'm lighter."

"No way."

Jessie glanced angrily at Sean.

He smiled back. "Remember what happened the last time you went first?" Sean reminded her.

Jessie looked at him, then shrugged. She couldn't argue with that logic, and they didn't have time to discuss it. Reluctantly she handed him the rope.

It took them only a few minutes to get ready. First Sean knotted a nylon-web sling around a nearby rock. Then he clipped the rope to the makeshift anchor.

Jessie pulled the rope taut, then looped it around her shoulders. She braced her body to lower Sean in a classic belay.

"Go for it, Sean," she called.

Sean gave her the thumbs-up sign. "Just like the climber on ESPN."

He stood at the edge of the cliff, holding the rope, his feet spread wide. He took a deep breath, gave Jessie a weak grin, then slowly backed over the edge and inched his way down the precipice.

Foot by foot he lowered himself to the plane, the harsh wind battering him from side to side. Finally he reached the rocks where the wrecked fuselage was wedged.

Sean lowered himself a few feet farther and peered inside the broken window. His heart leaped when he saw the familiar figure curled up in a corner.

"Dad!" Sean cried.

Eyes half closed, Jake lifted his head. "Sean . . . no," he rasped weakly. "Stay away. The plane's slipping."

"I'm gonna get you out of there," Sean said. He climbed onto the rock and put one foot on the plane's fuselage.

The weight of his foot caused the plane to shift dangerously, metal groaning.

Hurriedly Sean unclipped the rope from his climbing harness and began feeding the end of the rope through the open door.

"Tie this around you," he shouted over the wind.

Renewed energy surged through Jake's battered body. He grabbed the rope and nodded at Sean. Jake quickly looped the rope around his body, but his frozen fingers had trouble making a knot.

Jake looked up and spotted the two square yellow metal rings clipped to Sean's climbing belt. They were empty—which meant Sean had no lifeline.

"The ascenders," Jake croaked, pointing at Sean's belt.

Sean squinted. "What?"

"Your ascenders," Jake shouted weakly. "Those yellow things. Clip them to the rope."

Yellow things. Sean looked down and saw the yellow metal rings on his belt. Sean clipped one square ring to the rope and the other to his harness. It was a vital connection.

Metal creaking, the plane shifted down a long inch. With his stiff fingers, Jake still couldn't tie a knot, and he was running out of time. The wind was shaking the fuselage from its flimsy perch. Even the slightest wrong move would send the plane hurtling down to the rocks two thousand feet below.

"Dad, hurry up!" Sean yelled as the plane lurched another inch. He clung to the rock face, ready to reach down and grab his father. But Jake didn't appear.

He was still trying to knot the rope around his waist. Finally he managed to jam the rope through the loop and pull it tight. Jake bent forward to signal Sean.

Without warning the plane wrenched free and started falling down the frozen abyss.

Jake was yanked out the open door and swung from the rope like a broken puppet. Dangling above him, Sean gripped the single ascender with one hand as the plane spun wildly in the whirling gusts. It tumbled almost out of sight before smashing on the jagged rocks far below.

There was an enormous crash and a burst of flame. Then a thick black plume of smoke trailed up toward them.

Whipped by the high wind, Sean and Jake bounced off the rock face, spinning above the dizzying abyss.

Above them Jessie stood braced on the cliff's edge as the rope went taut with a *thwang*. Suddenly she was pulled off her feet and slammed hard against the anchor rock as her father's weight hit the rope.

Desperately she gripped the rope and got to her feet. "Sean? Daddy? Are you all right?"

No answer.

"Daddy?"

Sean and Jake were swinging dizzily in midair, unable to reply.

"I can't hold you," Jessie moaned.

That was not good news. Jake tried not to look down as he and Sean dangled in the howling wind. The problem was that he was deadweight. Maybe if Sean climbed up there to help Jessie . . .

"Sean! Clip the other ascender in!" Jake called. "Climb up the rope! Go on! Now!"

Sean hesitantly clipped the second metal ascender onto the rope. Dimly he realized how the yellow things worked. He shook loose the nylon sling and put his foot in it. This took the weight off the other ascender, and he began to slide up the rope.

Above him, Jessie strained to hold the rope, one eye on the coiled slack. There wasn't much left. Even worse, she was tied as final anchor. If she fell, they would all die.

What she couldn't know was that the nylon webbing slung around the rock behind her was slipping.

Sean spun around beneath the overhanging lip of the cliff, still scaling the rope using the ascenders. He slid the yellow rings up one at a time, while Jake hung on below him.

Sweat ran down Sean's face despite the bitter cold as he inched closer to the overhang.

Jessie dug her boots in, but the rope was slipping

134

faster through her trembling hands. She was so focused on looking over the edge that she never saw the danger behind her.

By the time Sean put one arm over the cliff's edge it was too late. The webbed anchor came untied, whipping Jessie around. Screaming, she was jerked to the ground toward the edge of the abyss, while Sean and Jake dropped ten feet.

The sudden stop jolted Jake's spine with paralyzing agony. "Jessie, hold on!" he cried.

Still gripping the rope, Jessie was dragged headfirst to the cliff's edge and certain oblivion. "Never give up," she chanted desperately, scrambling to grab hold with her boots.

But the rope was running swiftly through her numb hands. When the last remaining slack pulled tight, it would yank her over the edge. The three of them would fall to a horrible death. Their entire family . . .

"Sean! Help! I can't hold on!" Jessie screamed as the abyss yawned below her.

CHAPTER 21

An inch from the edge Jessie jerked to a stop.

She blinked in dazed disbelief, her breath smoking in the frigid air. Ever so slowly, unwilling to tip the balance by moving, Jessie glanced over her shoulder.

Behind her, standing stiff-legged, the rope looped in his jaws and his claws dug deep into the ground, was the young bear.

"Cubby!" Jessie sobbed gratefully.

With one last major effort Sean managed to heave himself over the cliff's edge. He threw himself on the rope and grabbed it tight. As he struggled to his feet he saw Cubby. The young polar bear was adding his weight to the balance.

Sean and Jessie began to pull their father's limp body up the cliff face. Even with Cubby's weight tipping the scales, it was hard, exhausting work. Straining with all their might, they hauled Jake up the cliff wall foot by foot.

Charged by their determination, Jake ignored the pain and used his good leg and one hand to help. Finally, after what seemed like hours of grueling effort, he got one shoulder over the edge.

Sean and Jessie grabbed their father's good arm and dragged him onto firm ground.

"Daddy!" Tears streaming, Jessie dived onto her father's chest, hugging him tight.

Despite his pain Jake draped an arm around her and squeezed. He closed his eyes. All through his ordeal Jake had never even dared to dream of this moment. Nothing could ever be better than this. His kids had done the impossible, and they had done it alone.

Then he saw Sean hanging back, his expression seeking unspoken forgiveness. Jake understood. He lifted his hand and pulled Sean in close. Jake kissed both his children, then raised his head.

"I just want to know one thing," he scolded gently. "What took you guys so long?"

He grinned and so did the kids, but Sean was still troubled. "Dad," he said hesitantly, "before you left, I said something—"

"Don't worry, I didn't hear it," Jake said, his voice husky with emotion. He pulled Sean closer for another embrace.

Jake heard a loud grunt. He turned and saw the bear sitting on his haunches. Flabbergasted, Jake shook his head. "Either that's a polar bear—or the whitest dog I've ever seen," he said in disbelief.

The bear stared back as if annoyed at being excluded from the family reunion.

"It's a dog," Sean said, grinning at Jessie. "Can we keep him, Dad?"

Sean was interrupted by the chopping sound of rotor blades. They all looked up as Charlie's helicopter swooped over the ridge.

"Hey!" they all shouted in unison. "Over here!"

Sean and Cubby sprang into action. Sean ran to get a smoke flare from his pack, while Cubby scampered to the top of the ridge.

Jake's eyes bugged out with surprise as he watched his son skillfully prepare to light the dangerous flare.

"Whoa! Sean!" Jake called weakly. "Let me do that."

Sean and Jessie looked at each other, then back at their father. "Dad," Sean said with a trace of exasperation, *"this* is nothing."

He grabbed the string and got set to launch the flare.

At first all Charlie saw was the plane wreckage spread across the ice. Certain that Jake was dead, he started back home. But as he swung around he spotted something odd on the far ridge.

A polar bear cub was standing on its hind legs, paws raised as if waving at him.

Charlie started to chuckle and flew closer. "Hey, little guy," the pilot muttered. "How'd you get up there?"

His smile faded when he saw the thick plumes of orange smoke billowing from behind the ridge. As the chopper flew over the crest, Charlie's jaw dropped open.

Three people were huddled near the rising cloud of orange smoke, shouting and waving frantically. When the chopper came closer, Charlie saw it was Jake, Sean, and Jessie.

"Oh, boy!" he muttered, fumbling for the radio mike. "You guys ain't gonna believe this," the pilot announced to the outside world.

Back in Quincy, the state trooper's office was jammed with people anxious for news. Word of Sean and Jessie's stay at Ben's camp had already reached the fishing village.

Sergeant Grazer manned the radio while his assistant, Harvey, sat nearby, munching on sunflower seeds. Behind them stood a number of Quincy locals, including Mrs. Ben and Captain Burl and his shipmates.

Sergeant Grazer had turned the volume up high so everyone could hear Charlie's report loud and clear.

"It's them!" Charlie said excitedly. "Jake and the kids! Sean and Jessie found him! On foot!" Charlie added, his voice croaking with disbelief. "They rescued him!"

The small office erupted with a wild cheer, causing Harvey to cough up his sunflower seeds. Mrs. Ben beamed at Sergeant Grazer, tears of joy glistening on her face.

The trooper's smile was part amazement and part admiration. "You have got to be kidding" was all he could say.

Soaring between the peaks, Charlie banked the chopper and circled lower, searching for a place to land.

When he neared the ledge, Sean and Jessie waved. Charlie gave them a thumbs-up sign out the window, his grin as wide as Alaska.

"Not bad for a couple of city kids!" Charlie laughed proudly.

Everyone back in Quincy had to agree.

Long miles away two men plodded across a bleak, unending wilderness. Bruised, battered, and angry, Perry and Koontz trudged silently, mourning their lost copter, lost skins, and lost profits.

Now we're lost, too, Koontz brooded. All because Perry had to chase after that bear cub. Well, he got him all right. That little beast did a lot of damage in a short time.

Koontz watched Perry limp painfully up a low ridge. Serves him right, the pilot gloated. He'll remember that bear for life.

Perry stopped and glared at Koontz. He still blamed Koontz for destroying their chopper. He shouldn't have slipped the safety on the shotgun, the hunter thought as Koontz neared.

"It's at least a week, maybe ten days to the nearest road," Koontz said.

Perry struggled to control his temper. The hunter's eyes narrowed, and he gripped his rifle, but he didn't reply as he limped along.

The pilot shook his head in disgust. "You had to go on chasing that bear, didn't you? 'I want him aliiive, Mr. Koontz,'" the pilot said, mimicking Perry. "'He must be aliiive.'"

Perry fumed, but still he said nothing.

"But I knew," Koontz continued, taunting him. "I told you that animal would be a lot easier to handle skinned, cleaned, and neatly folded."

Finally Perry turned to Koontz and gave him a look

bristling with hatred. "Yes, Mr. Koontz," he said, grinning slightly. "And so would you."

Koontz eyed the rifle in the hunter's hand and decided to shut up and keep on walking.

Charlie managed to land a short distance from the ledge, but carrying Jake to the chopper wasn't easy.

With Sean and Jessie's help, he slid Jake into the rear seat and strapped him down. Charlie grinned at his partner. "You're sure one lucky son of a gun."

Jake nodded at Jessie and Sean. "Yep, I sure am."

With Jake securely inside the chopper, Charlie helped Jessie and Sean get aboard. Exhausted, they slumped in their seats as Charlie slammed the door and throttled up the engine.

Then Sean remembered. "Wait," he said, pointing out the window. "What about Cubby?"

Charlie looked and saw the young bear sitting on his haunches, his expression mournful.

"Can we keep him? Please, Dad?" Jessie asked hopefully.

Jake shook his head. "Honey, he's a wild animal," he reminded her gently.

"Well, we can't just leave him, Dad," Sean said. "We owe him—big-time."

Jake noticed the air of calm authority in his son's manner. Sean had matured since he'd last seen him. Jake looked questioningly at Charlie.

Charlie shot a warning look at Sean. "Load him up," he said. "But if he tries to get in the front seat with me, I'm walking home."

As Sean jumped out of the chopper and ran over to

the bear, Jake said to Jessie, "That's funny. He called him Cubby."

Puzzled, Jessie asked, "Why? Who's Cubby?"

Jake smiled, remembering. "That was the name of his stuffed bear when he was a kid. Your mom gave it to him. He could never let go of the thing." Then Jake closed his eyes and slept.

CHAPTER 22

From the cockpit, high above the Arctic plain, the wilderness rolled out like a vast white carpet all the way to the blue peaks on a distant horizon. Patches of ice glistened like jewels in the bright sunlight as the chopper soared higher. The Barnes family had been waiting for perfect weather after Jake recovered from his ordeal.

The cast on Jake's leg and the tight bandages on his ribs made it slightly difficult for him to move around, but he felt very comfortable in the copilot's seat.

Charlie was at the controls, cruising at low speed to protect their precious cargo. Dangling from the chopper was a padded metal cage. Cubby was inside, swinging gently above the snowy landscape.

Jessie and Sean sat in the rear seat, staring down at the deserted plain. Jake and Charlie were also scanning the ground intently for any signs of life. Suddenly Jake spotted movement, but nothing more than a brief shadow. Jake tapped Charlie's shoulder and pointed. Charlie swung the chopper around lower.

Startled by the booming rotors, two white figures loped across the ice. A large mother polar bear had broken for cover, followed by her cub.

"Set her down beyond that ridge, Charlie," Jake said, pointing. If they landed out of sight, the bears wouldn't get spooked.

Charlie lifted higher, then eased the chopper down where Jake had suggested.

They all piled out, with Jake taking longest because of the cast on his leg. When he made it onto the ice, Jessie and Sean had already let Cubby out of his cage and were crouching beside him a short distance away. The bear sniffed the snow and nodded his head vigorously. Cubby was home.

Jake looked at his kids huddled around the wild bear and shrugged. He was still amazed by their deep bond, not to mention that Cubby had helped save his life.

"Well . . ." Jake gestured at the chopper. "We'll be waiting for you when you're ready to leave."

With Charlie, Jake limped slowly back to the chopper, glad he had remembered to bring a thermos jug of hot coffee. Just before he climbed into the craft, Jake took a deep breath. Cubby was right. The crisp Arctic air smelled great.

"You think he'll find a new family?" Jessie asked unhappily.

Sean nodded. He knew what his sister meant. "Yeah. He'll be okay. He belongs here."

Jessie knelt beside Cubby. The bear reached out and

laid a paw on her shoulder. She smiled, fighting back the tears.

"Good-bye, Cubby," Jessie whispered. She hugged the bear, pressing her face into his warm, silky fur. "You'll be okay, I promise. I love you," Jessie added huskily as she let go. She wiped away her tears with one hand and sprinted to the chopper.

Sean and Cubby looked at each other. The bear's soft brown eyes also seemed to be brimming with tears. But Sean knew what he had to do.

"Go on. Get out of here," Sean ordered, using his tough-guy voice.

Cubby didn't budge.

"Go on. You're free," Sean said, waving his hand. "Get a job. Get a life."

Cubby cocked his head at Sean. Then he reluctantly turned and padded away. Sean stood there watching him, trying to ignore his booming heartbeat.

Cubby paused and glanced back. Sean didn't move. The bear lowered his head and began lumbering across the snowy emptiness. Suddenly Sean's emotions burst through.

"Wait!" he yelled. He ran after Cubby and caught up. He reached into his pocket and pulled out a marshmallow pie.

Cubby gazed at him as if confused. Sean felt his eyes watering up. Quickly he unwrapped the treat and gave it to the bear. Cubby gobbled it down gratefully.

"Don't tell anyone . . ." Sean began, but his tears spilled over. He embraced the bear tightly, burying himself in Cubby's warm fur.

"Come back anytime if you want another," Sean said hoarsely.

Cubby pulled back and licked the tears from Sean's face.

When Sean returned to the chopper it was warmed up and ready to take off. Sean hopped inside and buckled up, smiling a secret, satisfied smile. Then he leaned forward and said to his father, "Let's go home, Dad."

Jessie reached out to embrace them both as Charlie gave them a thumbs-up and gunned the engine.

The chopper took off in a white swirl of snow, rising slowly into the shining blue sky. Sean looked out the window and spotted Cubby.

The bear stood on his hind feet as if offering a last farewell. Then he dropped down and padded over the ridge.

Immediately Cubby caught a familiar scent. He scampered down a snowbank and came face-to-face with another young bear—his size, his age.

Without any introduction the two cubs began romping happily in the snow—instant soul mates. They stopped playing when the mother bear trotted over. She circled Cubby warily, sniffing the newcomer.

Satisfied that Cubby meant no harm, she padded away toward the vast horizon.

After a moment's hesitation Cubby and his new brother followed her.

Behind them, Charlie's helicopter banked lazily over the ridge and began climbing into the sun.

ABOUT THE AUTHOR

FRANK LAURIA was born in Brooklyn, New York, and graduated from Manhattan College. He has traveled extensively and published eleven novels, including three best-sellers. He has written articles, short stories, and reviews for various magazines and is a published poet and songwriter. Mr. Lauria has also been an advertising copywriter and book editor. He currently resides in San Francisco, where he teaches creative writing. A film project based on his Doctor Orient series is in development.

WATCH OUT FOR...
BILL WALLACE

Award-winning author Bill Wallace brings you fun-filled stories of animals full of humor and exciting adventures.